Praise for
BODY FRIEND

'*Body Friend* is a kind of ghost story by stealth, an account of devotion, obsession and chronic pain that reveals a netherworld inside this one. It is told with such delicacy, with such a tender and insistent voice, that it becomes— uncannily, thrillingly—luminous.'
—**Miles Allinson, author of** *Fever of Animals* **and** *In Moonland*

'*Body Friend* is a deeply intimate tribute to the fragile and porous self, written in prose of rare clarity and tenderness. I felt everything reading this book.'
—**Claire Thomas, author of** *The Performance* **and** *Fugitive Blue*

'Brabon writes some of the most beautiful prose I've ever read, and this book is both muted and raw, like pain itself. A love letter to a body, to relationship and connection, and to water, Brabon explores what we need and how we need it with astonishing wisdom and candour.'
—**Laura McPhee-Browne, author of** *Cherry Beach* **and** *Little Plum*

'*Body Friend* is a remarkable and unflinching work that highlights, quietly and profoundly, the tedium and horror of living with chronic pain, but that also shows the lengths we go to understand ourselves, and to survive. Brabon's writing is important, and brave.'
—**Oliver Mol, author of** *Train Lord*

BODY FRIEND

BODY FRIEND
KATHERINE BRABON

Lines from 'In Plaster' from *Collected Poems* by Sylvia Plath used with permission from Faber and Faber Ltd.

Originally published in 2023 by Ultimo Press,
an imprint of Hardie Grant Publishing.
This edition published in 2024.

Ultimo Press
Gadigal Country
7, 45 Jones Street
Ultimo, NSW 2007
ultimopress.com.au

  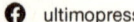 ultimopress

All rights reserved. No part of this publication may be reproduced, stored in a retrieval system or transmitted in any form by any means, electronic, mechanical, photocopying, recording or otherwise, without the prior written permission of the publishers and copyright holders.

The right of Katherine Brabon to be identified as the author of this Work has been asserted by them in accordance with the Copyright, Designs and Patents Act 1988.

Copyright © Katherine Brabon 2023

Body Friend
ISBN 978 1 76115 259 7 (hardback)

Cover design and illustration Allison Colpoys
Text design Simon Paterson, Bookhouse
Typesetting Bookhouse, Sydney | 13.2/19.3 pt Adobe Jenson Pro
Copyeditor Ali Lavau
Proofreader Rebecca Hamilton

10 9 8 7 6 5 4 3 2 1

Printed and bound by CPI Group (UK) Ltd, Croydon, CR0 4YY.

Ultimo Press acknowledges the Traditional Owners of the Country on which we work, the Gadigal People of the Eora Nation and the Wurundjeri People of the Kulin Nation, and recognises their continuing connection to the land, waters and culture. We pay our respects to their Elders past and present.

Late in the summer five years ago, when I was recovering from a surgical procedure, I met two women within a few weeks of each other and I saw both of them regularly, always separately, for some months afterwards. Summer did not give way easily that year, and even so we must force our bodies down to sleep in the heat, and even if experience does not give itself up easily to representation, I will lay it down anyway; frame the raw and exigent weeks, the untrustworthy months after the hospital, render it and them, Frida and Sylvia, as closely as possible to reality—or whatever is the feeling of a life and mind lived inside a body.

It was the first time I had lived in a room with a balcony and it was new, all of it: the act of opening the door, walking through, and still you did not leave the room. You stood instead in the air. And it was new, the way of seeing the street when it could not easily see you back. A balcony is part of your room and outside of it. It allows an external view without losing sight of the interior. It was a point of view in which I felt safe. The balcony was covered, so I could stand in the rain and my skin did not feel it.

We moved in February that year, Tomasz and I, into the large room on the second floor of a brick terrace share house in Parkville. We would split the rent with a student from the university nearby. We got the keys on a searing, still day and walked through the empty house. We sat on the balcony, drinking thin red wine from a mug Tomasz found in a kitchen cupboard, as the heat plateaued into the slow-coming dusk.

I thought that, from a distance, we must have looked young, like the university students who lived and sang at night in the surrounding streets. We would spend one last night at my old share house, and move all our belongings the next day.

That last night, the neighbours of my old house threw a party. At four o'clock in the morning, desperate for sleep, we got into Tomasz's car and drove to the new house—just a few streets away. The large old trees were haloed in streetlight, the eyes of a possum briefly struck bright by our presence. The empty rooms felt vast. The tall Victorian ceilings, the heavy wooden doors, carpeted bedrooms. We hadn't moved anything, none of our belongings except the large mattress from the house Tomasz shared with friends, and so we slept on it, low to the floor, that moonlit island the only object in the whole quiet house. We were exhausted; we left the blinds open. Outside, the plane trees—they call them London plane trees—moved a little. I slept deeply until the morning came quickly.

Soon after the move, I would be going to the hospital. The operation date had been set a year earlier, so there was nothing to do about the untimeliness of it. The doctor, Tomasz, my family, had all emphasised the need for the operation, had watched my limp gradually grow deeper, edging me closer to the ground as I walked, as my mind closed off from people, interests, opportunities, as I walked fewer steps each day.

After we woke in the empty house, I took painkillers and we stepped out into a morning of lingering heat, stopping for cold coffees on the way to my old house. After moving all of my belongings, we went to Tomasz's place and started with his. I couldn't really help with the heavy things—the desk or chairs or boxes of books. I could pick them up, hold them, but then walking was impossible. I apologised frequently. But the mood was light, during the moving days. We were happy with what we had decided on, living together.

In the new house, I noticed the closeness of strangers. I had never lived in a building that requires you to sleep so close to others, their bodies, the way terrace houses do, the way it is in the city, the way it must be in apartments all lined up like that. I grew up sleeping with silence, was raised on silence in a small country town, and yet when I return there now, to that blue, cold town, to the house of my parents, I cannot sleep because of the quiet.

Some nights we heard the young couple next door having sex. We laughed or muttered *shut up* as we heard one woman mostly (I guessed it was the one person), her high, loud moan. Some nights we heard the other neighbours, a middle-aged man and woman, arguing through the wall of our bedroom. The man was a gardener, he'd told Tomasz. They talked at the weekends, when Tomasz worked outside in the small workshop he made in the old Victorian-era outhouse, which stood in the small bluestone courtyard and in its share-house life had become a messy storeroom, the toilet long removed.

Since we were to use the mattress from Tomasz's house, I got rid of my old one, selling it cheaply online. A young woman and her sister came to collect it. One of their husbands arranged the sale. He assured me that the sister was strong, she could lift it. Once, on that mattress, I bled in front of Tomasz. I had slept naked, so had he. It was a deep sleep, we had been out drinking wine that night. We woke to a bed of brown blood; sheets painted in blissful, inebriated sex in the dark and then dried out while we slept. I thought by then that I had my body under control, knowing its cycles and the things that would happen. *It's okay*, he said. I bought new sheets, threw out the old ones. But the mattress was stained, and each time I stripped the sheets off I saw the telling mark, seeing it for the last time when I sold the bed to the young couple. The sister, a tiny woman with thin legs, hauled the mattress down the hallway by herself. The stain was there, a faded smudge of brown, and so my body's evidence persists somewhere, in someone else's night.

In the first days in that new house, the last before the surgery, I took a bath every night. I worked from home or took copious painkillers if I had to go to the office, and while there attempted to walk as little as possible, as I hated my limp and all that it signified.

I lay in the bathwater, which I would run extra hot, and let the weightless heat hold me. I heard Tomasz come through the front door downstairs, the familiar shake of keys, the ticking of bike wheels down the hallway.

'Food's on the stove,' I called. 'Should still be warm.'

I closed my eyes. I loved this time, the reunion and release at the end of a day. He ran up the stairs, light and quick. Bowl in hand, he walked into the bathroom.

'Dinner in the bathroom? On the toilet?' I was happy he was home.

'I'm actually doing it. It's gross.' He twirled the pasta with the fork, ate a few mouthfuls. 'I can't do this,' he said in mock indignation.

I laughed as he stalked back out of the bathroom. I turned to my side, the water lapped, he sat on the top of the stairs, eating and talking about his day. We were together between rooms. When the time came, he helped me out of the bath, his hands dry and warm.

Before the surgery I was in a halfway state. Not fully engaged in the world nor entirely detached from it. I was able to say: *I'll be going to the hospital soon*, or, *I'm not well today, I'm having surgery in just a few weeks*. I would not have readily admitted that I liked this time of stripped expectation, a lifting away of the public skin, but I did. I liked having a reason to excuse myself from what waits for us daily, the social outings or work commitments, even if that stripping away afforded me simply a moment to be by myself. This probably sounds terrible, even lazy. I don't know what people would think of this. But to my mind it is a positive act of refusal, a desire to reject something buried very deep in the structures we submit to in our lives. Perhaps calling myself lazy is a small fiction I don't really believe; my socialised self, the mask talking and accusing. Perhaps it's truer to think of participation in productivity as a small sidestep from oppression.

Tomasz became accustomed to the side of me that turned away from the world. In the lead-up to the operation, he spent more and more evenings at home. He even seemed to prefer it after a while, proclaiming exhaustion and declaring that he would rather work on his art projects in his workshop or put a movie on early in the evening. I was not sure if this progression in him was natural, a consequence of getting older, becoming less young, or if I caused this and if I did, whether that was a bad thing.

In the first years of our relationship we were constantly out, at bars, at restaurants, in parks with fizzing bottles, my body reasonably under control in that I'd not had a bad flare of the illness for some time, and Tomasz had not yet seen that side of me I knew lay dormant. That existence, the confidence to do those things, the bars, the parks, the long afternoons out and standing and walking, long and languid afternoons lasting until the late summer darkness arrived, in Edinburgh Gardens, in Princes Park, that faith in the body's capacity to withstand them, seemed now a series of brilliant moments, and any occasions like this I'd missed, which I did because of pain or introversion or fatigue, were a sign of thwarted potential I might never get back.

When we had not been dating long, when we barely knew each other in any deep way, I worried constantly that I wouldn't be able to keep up with him, or that I was stopping him from doing things he used to do often—the all-night parties, the spontaneous nights out. He seemed to do those things when I wasn't with him, and then when we were together he preferred to stay in, content to cook a meal and eat it on the couch in front of the heater, to fuck in the afternoon and maybe again before sleeping. *I send you to sleep*, I'd complain, *you're different when you're with your friends.* He would dismiss it, reassure me that he enjoyed this gentler pace, and yet I've always wondered how greatly we can shift the mundane and fundamental urges in a person.

And it seemed, in those days before the hospital, that my personality relented and curled into his care. I became almost infant-like, dependent and prone to express physically every need and emotion. The bad leg pained me constantly; I held on to walls to walk from one room to another. *My sick leg is so ugly*, I said to Tomasz, over and over again. *I hate this, my sick leg is so ugly.*

If I felt okay and cooked or stayed up late, days or hours afterwards it would come back to me, that energy spent, in a debt of increased pain and exhaustion that I couldn't help but see as retributive. Tomasz went out less. I would hear him say, *I think I'll stay in with her tonight*, and I would feel such relief I can't adequately describe it. Tomasz was a fixed safety, an enclosed, inviolable space in which I did sometimes dissolve into my teary fatigue or snap and rage at the pain before eventually settling.

His equilibrium was miraculous to me. It is still this way. His mood is even but playful, his energy always evident in the most truthful way. He is restless, he is active, he is tired, he is hungry, he is not hungry. Whichever he is, he is it fully; inhabits it fully and takes ownership of these needs. It is a great difference between us: I resist or am hypersensitive to bodily states, unable to meet them with acceptance whereas if he is hungry he will eat, he will not look at the clock like I would and say, *But it's too early* or *It's too late*. If I am tired, I seem to think this is wrong and push against fatigue, as though I've never needed to sleep, or I must sleep right then, now, or I'll cry. This difference is for me a source of envy but perhaps also love.

I don't pretend to be able to describe the pain experience. There is an argument that some things are beyond language, another that words are our only option. But I can say that before the surgery, what I felt was a ruling kind of pain, each shifting of muscles dictated by it. Every potential movement was interpreted by my brain in relation to that pain or its imminence, so that sudden movements—a stranger standing too close on the tram, an embrace from Tomasz—were provocations. I would be angry or heart-thumping or anxious at the perceived loss of control. To lose control of how I moved was to lose control of how pain materialised and was inflicted, which was to lose control of something yet more, one of those precious narratives that get us through our days, control tumbling out of and out of itself. Perhaps this last is the one we refer to when we simply say *lose control*. I was, have been, on high alert for years now. It is an odd vigilance the body keeps, the adrenaline to protect from potential hurt, some old and primal need activated and misused by the modern unwell body.

Autoimmunity is you and it's you against yourself and it creates invisible illnesses, except of course to the body they inhabit, except on the worst of their days. At the end of things—just before the operation, the only narrative end point I could construct at the time—when the pain was very bad, the illness emerged, as it were, visible to others after being, for so long, out of sight. In the final months, it was obvious that something was wrong with me. I would dress every day and put on make-up and blow-dry my hair, but I could not hide the limp as I walked past colleagues to go to the bathroom, to get a cup of watery coffee from the machine in the windowless lunchroom, as I walked into the classroom to face the students, as I got on and off the bus to and from the university. People seemed so surprised, even wronged, that I was *going in for* the operation. Surely not, I was too young for that. They shook their heads, rearranged their faces in a way that seemed to be both scrutinising me and disclosing their shock or even disbelief. They wished me well. In those situations I was almost glad to have some physical manifestation of the pain, as though I wouldn't have been believed otherwise. And so I left the university, the office, unable to see myself there on the other side of the surgical procedure. It was as if no one had made the same journey. Pain is incredibly singular. A disease of autoimmunity is you and you, you towards you, you against you, you with you, you upon you, you cannot extricate yourself, you cannot skin yourself off yourself—there is no such aftermath as a bodily divorce.

I was in the hospital for five days. I thought of myself as a young person having an old person's operation. I wasn't yet thirty and my joints needed replacing. The procedure seemed to go as it should, and the pain, with the deadening of strong medicines, was surprisingly minimal. The transitions were difficult. Home to hospital. The suddenness of a thin hospital gown on a naked body. Pre-surgery and the last moment staring into the anaesthetist's eyes, to the dissonant blur of awakening, stitched and raw. Horizontal immobility to standing, knocked by waves of low blood pressure. The surgeon ordered me to stay lying down for the first day after the operation, in case I fainted.

Throughout the first night, the woman in the bed next to me moaned for hours and spoke constantly of her pain. I asked the nurse if there was a private room. There were none, she told me, not unsympathetically. The next day I saw a young white boy, a teenager with blond hair, as he was wheeled post-surgery to the private room next door. I had missed my chance. The insurance to cover the surgery cost a hundred and thirty dollars a month. A person was required to be covered by the policy for one year—a year full of the constancy of painkillers, the limp I so hated—before claiming the procedure, and even then some extra thousands were to be paid directly to the surgeon, *un-coverable costs*, which I had in the bank only due to some book money, my first of that kind, and so I wondered if I'd been hoodwinked by this private insurance system with its surreptitious costs and unavoidable waiting.

Once, during those five hospital days, I had to go for X-rays. I had no idea what time of day or night it was. As I lay face up on the bed, skimming thoughts nowhere, two nurses came into the room and lifted me up using the sheets, one on either side to form a makeshift stretcher. They set me down on a bed on wheels and pushed it along the various corridors connected like limb and joint, turning wide and slow at each corner. We arrived in the X-ray area, signalled by ominous black-and-yellow signs with a windmill-like image warning of radiation danger. For whatever reason—perhaps it was a busy time—the nurses left me. I lay on the gurney, my palms facing up, in the empty corridor. Soon I was desperate for the toilet. I couldn't get up, I wasn't yet able to stand without help, and there was nobody nearby.

A terrible loneliness in that moment: fluorescent, whirring air; chemically sharp, clean floors; a body waiting and needing. When I was finally taken back to the ward, lifted again with the sheets and onto the bed, when finally the nurse brought me the bedpan, pulled the sheet across like a magician covering up a secret process, the pan was close to full and I was too embarrassed to ask for it again during her shift. I learned when the nurses stopped and started, when I should wait or ask for things again, so as to avoid seeming too demanding.

It's frightening how quickly it became a home to me, how soon I was habituated to the cell of a bed, how it became a point of view in which I felt safe, the view of the tops of the buildings in Richmond, five days watching sunsets and reflected sunrises through glass, content that I would never be out there to see them. I liked the regularity of the early breakfasts, done by seven, the tea served mid-morning and then again mid-afternoon. The visits from various staff on their rounds—choose your lunch, your dinner, choose tomorrow's breakfast—and how strange it must be, then normalised, for their daily tasks to involve seeing someone in their most vulnerable, unselfed state. The conversations that took place around me, beyond the protective white curtain. Time passed in small deep sleeps of journeys to an ocean floor, and in visits from family and friends during which I felt a fragile, strange specimen in a white cloak, surrounded by loved faces who brought in the weather—summer, warmth on their cheeks; who brought in eyes and purpose from outside; who were suddenly slowed by the steady, focused quiet, convalescence, fluorescence, astringent air and fetid beds, the rise-and-fall of the hospital. Perhaps the enforced enclosure and stillness of a hospital validates for a time so many of our subversive, subterranean longings.

I became so accustomed to the routines of the hospital, to the noises and unending light denoting a knowing presence, to the people, almost always women, who brought tea and cereal, tea and biscuits, lunch and then more tea on a tray wheeled in on a trolley, to the sealed view of an east-facing sky above the suburbs to my left, the thin white curtain making a permeable wall to my right and separating me in quite a pointless way (I could hear her breathing, her swallowing, her body's fluid gurgling after eating; how did sight make a difference?) from the person next to me. I didn't drink coffee for five days, my body didn't want it, and I was entirely dependent on others.

I was told that I was ready to go home, after the five days my surgeon predicted.

Tomasz helped me into the car, I used the crutches we had purchased because to hire them would likely end up more expensive, a fact I railed against, while Tomasz told me it was fine, relax. *And who knows*, said the consulting physiotherapist, *you might need them again someday*, a statement I likewise resented and repeated to Tomasz after the woman left. Outside, the day was bright and I noticed the fresh air, the smell of jasmine and exhaust fumes. A kind of jet lag, and strange, to be in a different time from others going about their workdays. I was removed from all that, a state both freeing and constrictive, bound up as it was with my ideas of choice and control, how illness could come through and steamroll both things, while perhaps shedding light on other truths, and how there may be a hesitant freedom within yourself in this state while you nevertheless try to operate in the more restrictive structures of society and economy around you. I think all this in retrospect, of course. On that trip home I contemplated only banalities: the steep stairs in the house; whether I'd be able to sleep; how long Tomasz would stay home with me while I recovered.

And so when the nights felt new in the house—my first time living with Tomasz, with any boyfriend—the nights in my body also felt new. The transitions were difficult, I've said this already. Hospital to home: perhaps the most difficult adjustment. I was aware of the presence of the new, artificial joint, the strange absence of pain where it was once so intense. Other pains emerged in place of the absent one. The leg that wasn't used properly (the limp, the bent-over posture), manifested the ache of atrophied muscles now pulled suddenly long and taut, as the aberration of my hip joint disappeared just like that. The muscles, years shrunken, had the sudden pain of overuse, as though I had run great distances when I had barely moved. Habituation, atrophy, learned behaviour, guardedness: words were spoken as though my body had done those things without me. It had learned to walk unevenly. The muscle had become slack, even lazy. My uneven gait was as much from necessity at the joint wearing away as it was an act of protection, a guarding mechanism. All such things happened to the body and mind as though done behind my back, apparently, or while I was sleeping.

In the new, raw days after I returned from the hospital, Tomasz wanted to help me with even the smallest tasks, to do nearly everything for me, as though my time in hospital was completely incomprehensible to him, transforming our intimacy so that my capacities or impotence were now unknowable. I hated this; *I can pick up my own cup, for god's sake, Tomasz.* I was tired all the time, and angry much of it. He wanted me to be better, I thought, he was almost impatient for it. In my head I accused him at times, declared him guilty of the impatience I perceived behind his care. Though mostly I didn't blame him. I was aware of illness's capacity for the transference of emotion, that the impatience I attributed to him might in fact lie in me. We took a few walks. There was a cafe less than three minutes from our house; now it took us at least seven minutes. But it was nice to go there with Tomasz, who sometimes looked at me with a bewildered expression, as though I had become unfamiliar to him.

    He returned to work after a week, leaving the house in the morning just after eight and returning around dinnertime. Convalescence, an old-sounding word, a good word, it rises and falls from the tongue like its meaning. It is a state to be in, a state of being. Convalescence, suggesting a passage leading beyond it: harmless, really; a temporary allowance of time during which we are healing, cared for, and do not need to go outside. Those days passed slowly and yet a week went by all in a rush and blur. The quiet of the noon lunch hour shocked me. I ate alone, hearing the scrape of metal on porcelain. The wound—boundary between internal and external, violated privacy—was healing. I was scared to look at it. A nurse visited to change the dressing once a week. When I pulled down my trousers and underpants, squatting over the toilet because it was hard to sit down, I was terrified of a finger hooking the gauze, tearing it off and reopening the wound.

Despite these small terrors and lonelinesses, the days were peaceful. I even had time to love them, to love the singularity of that time meant for healing. I confessed to no one that the thought of returning from that state was frightening. I didn't know to what I was returning.

As I looked ahead, past that time of convalescence, to an elusive state called *better*, *well*, a fresh-air place, it seemed an unknown location. I was suspicious of the narrative, hesitant to place trust in any process that promised cure. In many ways the recovery was a place as liminal as the months before the surgery. Initially, after the hospital, Tomasz was in that state with me. Even after he went back to work, he came home earlier than usual in the evenings. And like before, I would take baths before bed, and he'd join me in the water, glancing sometimes at the healing scar on my upper thigh, high up near the groin. We'd lie there, bodies splayed before each other, alternating the position of our legs so that we could take turns submerging our shoulders and neck in the water. Tomasz would scrunch his eyes closed, take a long, deep breath, and put his head under the water, and I'd laugh at the childlike abandon with which he'd do this and then emerge with a wide-eyed gasp, dripping mouth, saying, *How long was that?* He would get out first, dry off, and then stand there naked, holding a towel and waiting for me to step my good leg out first, then the bad one (*it's not bad anymore, it's healing,* he would say), a benign seriousness on his face, and the outright exposure of both of us then—my vulnerability, his worry, the two of us naked and damp—was a brief moment I knew we'd somehow return to when we were older, or perhaps with another person, in our later lifetimes.

Gradually Tomasz started going out again. He would say, *Is it okay for me to meet so-and-so tonight, will you be okay here?* He sometimes asked if I wanted to come too, although we both knew I would be asleep by dinnertime, that I would wake as often as a baby in the night. I alternated between heavy sleeps, fatigue, and insomnia, a confluence of the lingering effects of the anaesthetic and the pain of my bad leg adjusting to being used properly again. Admittedly I did not want him to leave, though I never said so and knew such thinking was irrational, even unfair. Those first weeks after I left the hospital created a space I did not want either of us to leave. I hadn't yet gone outside by myself. At the same time I didn't want him to ask permission, didn't want all that carefulness, that eggshell existence.

I said I wished I could go out, to drink wine, to sit in a bar. I said it more and more, as I watched him return to normal life.

We can, Tomasz would say. *There aren't any rules.*

Not yet, I would always say. According to some self-constructed regulation, a repetitive thought, I told myself I could go out a month after the surgery. It seemed absurd, wrong somehow to pretend that things were back to normal. Or excessive, against some moral norm, to go out drinking wine, to think about such a thing as sitting in bars, when I was so close to that time in the hospital. As though I hadn't yet crossed some threshold of recovery. We invent these states, to a degree, and I was desperate to leave while at the same time clinging to interiority, convalescence, for a while longer. I was full of these kinds of contradictions, any neat demarcations of want and need and capacity lost in the states of being I'd inhabited since I first got sick, when I was twenty.

After five weeks, the doctor said I was ready for the pool, as though it were a rite of passage I was finally fit to undertake. The scar from the surgery was healing. Stitches dissolved. Skin taut, stretched, and bothered by the incision and the opening to make way for the work underneath it. The surgeon, who was surprisingly young and kind and had green eyes, sent me to a physiotherapist he knew. This man, the physiotherapist, held rehabilitation classes in a pool.

You are told things at times in your life. I was told, by people who must have known, that it was ill-advised to look at what the operation I'd had involved. I should not search for videos and evidence; I should not witness the wide-stretched skin, the sawing of joints, the chunk of bone, an entire component you were born with, removed, discarded and replaced. There were many thresholds, I was learning, with a body that is bad and then good and then bad again. I was told when I was ready for things and when I had to wait for things. I was ready for surgery. I was ready to return home. Then I was ready for the pool.

The specialist pool was on a side street near St Vincent's Hospital in Fitzroy.

I bought a cheap black bathing suit at Target, telling myself there was no point in buying anything special as I doubted my propensity to keep up the act of swimming. I tried it on at home, practising the careful stepping inside of each leg opening, holding the fabric wide to avoid the healing scar. Tomasz lay in bed, reading something on his phone.

'What do you think?' I said with what I hoped was light indifference.

He looked up. 'Hot. Turn around.'

I laughed and went to the bed. He moved his hands over the silky black polyester, a second skin, and kissed me.

At first it was confronting: the stripping down, the body cold, the cold shower, the cold gasp of the pool. My scar still raw. The physiotherapist said the body had to be eased back into the water, as though we'd been wombed there, were now meeting some primal return. And he was a nice person, the physiotherapist, which made it easier, made it harder, to be in pain in front of him.

In the past week I'd progressed to walking alone each day to the cafe near our house. Sometimes I walked with crutches, more often with a single crutch as a buffer against panic. Tomasz called me less often from work during the day, which I took as a sign that I seemed better. I even cooked sometimes, feeling oddly energised and faint from standing for so long. In tired moments I was horrified that I still limped, I almost cried about it, even if the limp was mostly righted, now just a faint unevenness. It annoyed me that I'd had such faith in what I saw as being fixed, faith delivered into the perceived potential of the surgery.

The physiotherapist walked through the water and spoke to each of us, offering direction, suggestions for movements, actions to repeat over and over, encouraging the body to move in ways that on land it struggled to accomplish. In my case, repetition in pursuit of symmetry in the body. Dripping, I walked the distance between shower and pool, limping slightly, feeling exposed and vulnerable, and I remembered my sister at three days old, as my father held her over the infant bath, dipping her gently in and under. The way her arms curled and shook with questions, *what is this, this air, this gravity*, and how, when he lowered her into the warmth, she looked up with calm eyes, eyes three days opened, as if she had been returned safely.

I left the hydrotherapy classes feeling tired, feeling a strange sense of transcendence, a great relief in my body. I was tired because of the body, but not its pains or its thinking mind, and there was such absolution in this. Our bedroom upstairs seemed unaccountably peaceful. The walls, a smooth and greenish white, reflected their cool stability on my skin. Tomasz put on a film and it seemed such a wonderful, uncomplicated time as I lay in my body, as if the nerve endings were cloaked and finally safe. I wanted to touch Tomasz, his face and his ears and his arms. My body after water: lightness with an abstruse feeling of forgiveness, as if I'd reached a moment when I'd done nothing wrong.

I went back to the pool the next week. All of us—the other patients, whom I now recognised, and me—followed our instructions, floated and kicked, moved and then were still, each a small and separate island. The others in the class were either young or old. We were all in various stages of recovery or ill-health. The two Italian women in their seventies who always tied and untied their shoes together, who struggled to reach and put on their socks. The young woman, perhaps younger than me, with scars from what I guessed were several surgical procedures. She seemed strong, an athlete, she had many tattoos and she moved through the water like she knew it. Some people, I noticed, moved well in water, their movements fluid and dense. Others moved well on land. The physiotherapist was a runner, marathons, and I had the sense that he didn't love being in the pool. It was a necessary healing tool for his patients, an intermediary step so that they might return to land.

I became aware of a woman in the pool. I noticed her because of certain similarities. She had hair like mine, long and blonde-auburn, and was also around thirty years old. Outside of the water, she had a faint limp like mine. You could have said *she was shaped just the way I was*, like Plath writes in her poem about a plaster woman, another version of herself. I wondered, an impossible question, if we had the same pain.

    We all got out of the water, in our own time and private little miseries. The woman who seemed to be like me glided serenely and then walked up the few stairs out of the pool. The moment she was on land she was unsteady, found things to hold on to—a chair back, a handrail—as if scared she might lose her balance.

I tried not to watch her. I couldn't help myself. I looked at her knee joints, their flesh uneven from swelling and fluid, and how pain seemed to follow the movements of her neck and head. She could not turn her head far without moving her whole body. Her torso was long, as were her arms and neck, an olive tan on her arms and chest. Her legs were shorter in comparison, the skin paler. She had large brown eyes and her damp hair turned dark blonde, almost brown. It was like watching a distant mirror.

I was not looking for someone just like me. I did not seek the doppelgänger, that object of cultural obsession. Meeting your likeness is said to be an omen; the world only has room for one of you. My fascination with the pool woman was not a vanity, I need to stress this. It was maybe an exercise in self-knowledge.

I don't think we ever want that badly to find ourselves mirrored in another person. We want enough similarity not to be alone, enough difference to know ourselves. While we might be able to share emotional suffering, either experiencing some element of it ourselves or feeling something close to what the other does, anger or sadness or despair, in a practical sense another's physical pain can never be ours. I don't know if I can explain it. When I see bodies in pain, I feel what could be called nothing for them. I can sympathise but I can never actually feel that pain, just as nobody can ever really feel mine. Even if I am watching those I love most in agony, I feel hurt because of the emotional suffering that pain brings or simply the knowledge that pain exists in them. I do not experience their physical suffering, in the common conception of empathy being the capacity to feel another's pain. I think this might be a truth. Bodies hold the exactness and veracity of pain, and we use their metaphors because pain is woven tight to the self. *It burns, it's killing me*, but it doesn't, it isn't. Approximate always, the metaphor. *I feel your pain* means: *I feel bad because you are in pain*. Since I had been with Tomasz, entwined absolutely in so many gratifying ways, I was nevertheless acutely aware of this unavoidable distance.

Watching this woman was different. It was a strange sense of identification. With this mirror woman I didn't feel her pain but rather I knew it, because it was also mine. Towards her pain I felt the same banal familiarity I had towards my own. I knew the physicality but, more deeply, I knew the mental patterns associated with her pain, though the two pillars of perception might have been impossible to differentiate. I knew that she felt a grating anger at the pain in her neck and her knees, that she did not want strangers to walk too close to her. I knew her vigilance and the enormous weightlessness permitted by painkillers and, now, by water. I was inexplicably certain of these things about her. Considering how close, how unstoppably absorbed we became, as two people, in hindsight it is incongruous that our first meeting was so brief and impersonal. In the changing room, she looked at me with her large brown eyes, offered a small smile, and left.

I started to go often to the pool near St Vincent's Hospital. The rehabilitation building, and inside it the hydrotherapy pool, adjoined the hospital and was accessed around the corner from it. The hospital stood on a small rise in Fitzroy, as churches often stand on the highest point of elevation. From the hill there was a heavily interrupted view, across suburbs and tall commercial buildings, of the Dandenong Ranges forty kilometres away.

The woman who seemed to be like me waved in recognition as we got out of the pool. After showering, we stood near each other in the changing rooms and dressed in silence. By now I was used to seeing the naked bodies of the people around me. It hadn't taken long for me to shake off unease at my own nakedness and expose myself freely, a liberation I didn't know was in me. In the changing rooms I noticed a respectful looking away, everyone occupied by their own acts of drying and dressing, so that we each shrank our sphere of attention and the room became a rare space of demarcation, a removal of the obligation to look and engage. Yet most of them, the women who went to hydrotherapy, nevertheless kept talking, socialising, commiserating and sharing, all the while focused on their own bodies, drying and moisturising and changing. The woman and I finished dressing and packed our sodden towels and bathers into our cloth tote bags at the same time. We left the pool building together and turned the corner. At the small kiosk at the entrance to the hospital, she asked, 'Are you in a hurry?'

We ordered coffee and sat on the hard plastic chairs near the kiosk. A young nurse ate his lunch from a plastic container. The woman seemed ravenous for her coffee and tried to drink it straightaway, blowing and carefully bringing the cup to her lips.

'I'm Frida,' she said. When she smiled, thin wrinkles formed around her eyes. She pushed up the sleeves of her lightweight woollen jumper, and brought her hands together. She wore jeans and sensible-looking casual shoes. When she folded one leg over the other, her foot jiggled with energy.

Frida asked if I liked the pool, if I had always been a swimmer. I told her that, like most children at my school, I'd had swimming lessons. I did well once at a school swim carnival, even won a few ribbons, but it had been years. Now was different, and new. I told her how my joints felt light after the pool, so light I didn't care about my thoughts, I could have stayed in the water forever. I felt some new connection to the routines and associations of the pool. I hadn't yet found the words for it. Probably I was gushing, in the way I sometimes let things go with strangers.

She laughed. 'You're hooked.'

I laughed too. I was light, so light, the swimming made me feel all body, only body, my new and best painkiller, a dose of cool limpidness across the skin, like water.

Often when we meet someone, we have to, or feel we must, begin the task of creating ourselves yet again, offering a narrative that presents us as we hope to appear, perhaps as we hope we are. I struggled with this. On any ordinary day I felt so different from one moment to the next, alternately introverted or talkative, bright then withdrawn, apparently a writer but more concretely a student. And most of all I was always unsure whether to mention the illness, a difficulty that felt even more pronounced after the surgery, with no certainty as to what constituted *better* or *good*; precisely, how to integrate the state of the body into identity? But with Frida I didn't need to. I thought this might be because of the pool: we had known our bodies before speaking to one another and so they had, our bodies, made a blissfully shapeless mark on the canvas of the self presented to the world. We didn't mention our illnesses on that first occasion. Perhaps the most striking sign of this lack of compulsion to draw myself in a certain way in front of Frida was that I felt under no strain or social obligation to be nice or overly engaging. I did not smile so much and this made me calm.

'It's good to be in the pool with someone like me,' Frida said. 'Someone my age. I thought I would be the odd one out.'

We ordered a second coffee, we were light-headed, happy, and she said, more than once, *But you are just like me.* I thought it too. I said to her, *But you're just like me.* We laughed. We were like schoolgirls who have claimed each other: you're my best one.

During the pool sessions, the physiotherapist gave us each a set of exercises, their levels of difficulty and exertion dependent on our state of healing or pain: walk up and down the stairs in the pool; stand at the edge and squat repeatedly while holding the rails; lean your back and arms against the pool edge and pedal as if on a bicycle; walk from one end of the pool to the other, back and forth, and again. The two older Italian women stood together at the edge and held the rails, squatting up and down slowly, up and down, so that the water came over their shoulders and then receded as they stood again. The young athlete with the tattoos stalked determinedly back and forth; she looked straight ahead and never made eye contact with anyone, her face contorting every now and then. *Go easy*, the physiotherapist told her, *don't overdo it*. She pasted him with a glance and again looked straight ahead, focusing on her exercises.

Hydrotherapy as faith in water, its capacity to relieve us of the weight of our bodies, the heaviness of being every day on the earth. This freedom from gravity, the inadvertent gift of water, was still new to me. The body could move, step, dance as was not possible on land.

I began to love the pool. I got out of the water, dried my skin, wrung out my bathers, clenched my hair dry and walked to the tram stop to go home. On land I wondered when I might go back into the water again. I counted the hours until that moment and marvelled at the way the body in water is always a return, always returning to weightlessness.

Often, the physiotherapist gave Frida and I the same exercises, and we moved like mirror images of the other. Frida lifted one arm and I lifted the other. I lifted one arm and Frida lifted the other. She walked from one end of the pool to the opposite side, I walked across from the opposite direction. We passed at the midpoint. We rested together with our backs to the edge, arms outstretched, bodies cruciform.

Frida turned to me. 'My legs are no good.'

'And my legs are no good,' I said back to her.

'Do you want to walk with me?' she asked afterwards, as we dried our hair. The autumn days were cooler and it was no longer possible to let the warmth of the breeze and sun dry our dripping heads.

We walked together out into the brisk air and with it the feeling of deliverance and effacement, after the humidity, after water. We walked past the hospital and the kiosk, along the wide street divided by tram lines. The trees, the emerging autumn shades, the trams, all passed us, but we went as far as she could, as far as I could, our legs were no good, we both said this as we walked, we comforted each other with these little mantras. I feel this. I feel this, too. Frida told me she had become stronger because of the water. It was a narrative I could believe in.

Frida spoke with such devotion about the pool and her physical movement. She had been diagnosed with an illness—*the illness*, she called it, and we started to use this singular, definite form between us—in her early twenties, but it wasn't until recently that she'd realised exercising aggressively, she said it in that way, aggressively, helped her symptoms. She felt better, she felt renewed.

It was easy to become obsessed with the pool. It was forgiving of every bad day, it made me forget any food I should not have eaten, any wine I should not have drunk, the days I didn't move enough, which made my joints, my legs, my arms like stones. Frida felt the same way. We felt many of the same things.

Around this time, in the early months after the hospital, I met up with friends at a bar in Ascot Vale. It was the first time I had been out by myself at night since before I was in the hospital. I did not take the crutches with me. The physiotherapist said it was time I stopped relying on them. My brain and muscles would become too accustomed, he said, which was as good as saying I'd be emotionally dependent on them. There was a balance, he said, between working my body too much and too little. He warned me against upsetting this balance that seemed determined by an invisible scale.

Tomasz was working late, so the house was empty and quiet as I got ready to leave. The walls felt high and startling, in the way a place you know can become estranged from you, and in the coldness of the still rooms I wondered if it was too late to cancel. I'd been happy to make the plans, truly; even excited. But as though another person, another woman, had made them, I was very different, from whoever she was, in that moment, that very long and lonely hour. There was a good excuse waiting to be used—that the pain was bad, that it was too soon after the surgery—but then the time to leave arrived and there I was, walking very slowly down to the tram stop and then suddenly, too soon, the old tram trundled up, ready for me, and I was trying to look calm as I gripped the handle, went up the too-high steps, one, two, three, all with the right leg first, right, right, right and up, because the left leg was weak, then held the arm rail carefully, carefully, and mercifully found a seat. I avoided looking at anyone near me in the carriage. The same ordeal to get down the stairs again, then a few steps to the bar, just beside the tram stop.

Inside, the furniture was made of dark-stained wood, the walls white, the light mellow. The friends said I should choose the wine. I stood with the bartender for a long time, talking over the vast wooden expanse of the bar, as if across a still lake in the middle of the night, reciting my friends' various preferences, which I was trying to accommodate, until she said, *So they let you choose but you don't really have a say.* Finally I ordered something and returned to the table. Two of my friends had recently had a daughter together. They looked often at their phones, at her small body sent in pictures by the babysitter.

They asked me in gentle ways about the book I was writing, or was supposed to be writing before the surgery.

They knew that lately I had felt distanced from the act of writing. I found the divide between the writing self and the self talking about writing an increasingly intolerable chasm. In the case of the latter, I was not who I felt to be. I had hoped to create something that would act as a bridge between these selves, but had lately stopped altogether.

My friend told us the story of the time she created a fake online profile. She did this so she could view her real profile from the position of a stranger. She wanted to see how she seemed, what she looked like from the outside, from the perspective of others, and so she created a persona, another woman. She even gave this woman a name and an indistinct photograph she'd found online of a woman whose features were similar to her own. It was an interesting exercise in self-reflection. Superficially it was hard to distinguish such acts from vanity, but I sensed that in the case of my friend her actions instead had their beginning in a buried sadness, a desperate desire to know herself.

'Through her,' my friend said, 'I could see how other people saw me.' She laughed. 'It was weird. I sort of felt like she was real, like I knew her.'

'Oh yes, I remember her,' her husband said. 'I think I added her as a friend.'

My friend turned to me. 'Perhaps you need to create a persona, a woman like you, a character who reflects you to yourself, to have a sense of how you are perceived from the outside.'

BODY FRIEND

I wasn't convinced this would help me know myself better;
I would only know my projected self.

They all agreed that the wine was good.

In the mornings I stood on the balcony and crushed paracetamol with my back teeth. The tilting wooden boards creaked and groaned. Over the ornate wrought-iron lacework, three tall ginkgo trees stood along the footpath in front of the house. The large London plane trees shaded the green traffic island that cleaved the street in two. During those months of recovery I sat on the balcony in the mornings, every morning, up with the ginkgo leaves. They were green then and so bright, during the limited window of sunlight before it passed over to the other side of the house. I saw Tomasz leaving for work, riding his blue-grey bike, headphones in his ears. He had left behind our shared morning, couldn't hear or see me up there on the balcony. His day had begun. I saw him while he had no knowledge of being seen.

I aligned my body with Tomasz's, in the early days, when we first met. When he would move his body, ride his bike, commute to work, I would join him. If he slept in, then I would try to do the same, even though I've never been able to sleep through any morning. And I aligned my body to his hunger. Hunger as perhaps our original pain. Though conscious of participating in clichés of gender, I would not say I wanted to eat, was embarrassed, needing too much, was sure of it. And so we would have coffee first thing and only later, hours towards lunch, would we eat. Often I didn't know if I was hungry and yet I ate at the designated times. Hunger by the minute hand's salivation. There was some murky shame behind this, some inkling that our capacity to eat when we are not hungry is our greater hunger, our great undoing, danger and sadness, our signifier. Only some animals do this, become gluttons when they live with us. The birds who cannot stop pecking, pecking at their seed because it's there, all there in front of them. The cats who eat until they vomit. They need us to stop them eating and they need us to feed them. We are the same but we are the hand that feeds us.

Perhaps I aligned myself with Tomasz's body because his seemed to me to be good. As though I wanted to find another body to live by, because mine could only do wrong. Doctors were surprised at the tenacity of the illness. *It's aggressive*, they would say, and then they'd write the same in my file: *a severe and aggressive manifestation.*

I had started to think to myself that perhaps the body was the most honest of us all. Honest, because when the body dies, so do we, in the sense of how we know a person, but the same cannot be said of language. We can lose our narrative and somehow our bodies still survive. And conversely, when our bodies die our stories can possibly continue, if we have carved them in stone. The body is an original state, and for this reason it is honest or true, while narrative comes after, is always a created, secondary thing prone to sculpting, manipulation, artifice. Often we deny the body its story. We don't believe it or we ignore it, because the body does not use words. We ignore the body because sometimes we don't even know what it is saying, or we choose not to listen to its needs, this miraculous, silent carapace. It is nature, in this sense: body as landscape, climate, fauna.

The illness, in some ways, gave me freedom from plot, from the social life's play-acting of self-constancy. It made me aware of myself as a pure organism, discrete and living, composed of cells changing and dying and renewing. Our physical bodies shed themselves, the skin that makes or contains us, thousands of flaking dead things by the minute. All we keep are our hair and our nails until they, too, break and fall. And yet we assume that our non-physical correlate either stays the same or is fixed enough for narrative.

You've got a different body, an old boyfriend said to me once. I hadn't seen him for years. We were in the small cold town where I grew up, where we'd met. Sixteen and summer and first sex which tumbled into years together, early adulthood. He hadn't seen me since I'd become sick and lost weight, lost my periods and breasts, when I was first sick and the disease was so active, the body so inflamed it burned through everything I ate, leached me of any nourishment, even after I'd stopped eating certain foods to try to make myself better. My legs were thinner than they'd ever been. *It's a different body*, he said, resuming in seconds the intimacy we'd had years ago, collapsing time in the way possible with some old relationships. I didn't reply, *You've got a different soul.* A person just doesn't say things like that.

And so I stood on the balcony and crushed paracetamol with my back teeth. Two tablets at a time, six tablets per day. I crushed them because of my neck and its new pain, which had formed after the surgery, and with it some new fear that I'd choke if I tried to swallow those white pills. I thought it would be a temporary thing, I'd get over it, but we are terribly animal and train ourselves into these habits, and I couldn't stop the panic each time I put a tablet on my tongue and thought about swallowing it. And so I crushed them with my teeth, the pieces bitter and chalky, like plaster, and washed the granules down with coffee or water.

In my mouth I ground down the tablets, over and over, endless little machine. A magpie in the plane tree closest to me let out a single piercing call. *A severe and aggressive manifestation.*

At the pool, in the hydrotherapy class, we became a group. We knew each other. The young woman with tattoos, Frida, me. The two old Italian women who wore rubber sandals with velcro straps. I liked the gentle way they took their sandals off to change into their bathers, strapping them back on to walk from the changing room to the main pool. They took them off before going into the pool to do their exercises together. They put them on again to go back to the changing room. Each time they did so they had to sit, careful, slow and sore, to remove them, put them on again. They took them off to get changed. They put them on after getting dressed. And finally, after leaving the changing room, they took them off in the wide hallway, replaced the sandals with socks and black lace-up shoes. All that patience they had, through their stiffness and pain. I imagined these women in their homes, the repetition of their labours, the deliberate, gentle slowness of each task. I thought of quiet rooms and cold carpet, pristine kitchens with plastic-covered tables, coffee in the air and I wondered, perhaps unfairly, maybe with distorted romanticism, if the women were lonely in long marriages.

I saw Frida there every time, at the hydrotherapy pool in Fitzroy. Soon I simply associated the pool with her presence. She seemed to have such control, such order in her life. She worked at a university too, and I liked this similarity between us. I was impatient to recover and be like her. I hoped I could recover and be like her. We had coffee or walked after each visit to the pool. We were friends.

April progressed and the morning air was cold. I loved that I could think of deep autumn in that air. The cool yellow light, the wide blue sky, the skin relieved. Despite the cool mornings, the days were nearly hot, our first-floor room stagnant at night, the fan oscillating nonstop, and still the mosquitoes whining for blood. The ginkgo leaves outside our window turned slowly and then all of a sudden blazing yellow. Those nights I would lie awake thinking about every one of my bones, as if I knew them all, and wait for morning. I perhaps felt fear. And yet I thought of the woman named Frida, too, and she was like a happy and secret possibility inside me. And this calmed me; just the thought of her calmed me.

As we were leaving the pool one day, Frida invited me to visit her apartment in St Kilda.

'You can smell the sea, even if you can't see it,' she said. 'You'll have to trust me that it's really there.'

Frida met me at the train station the next afternoon and we walked together to her apartment. We walked at the same pace, each of us with a weaker leg, a faint limp. She wore loose-fitting clothes: black linen pants, a short-sleeved white shirt, and, despite the colder air, just a thin grey scarf and no jacket.

'I'll take you the long way around,' she said, 'so you can see the water.'

The large houses and apartment complexes on the Esplanade faced the bay. There was a boldness to their outlook. They were so open to the sea, from the balconies, the windows, the front doors, there was no way to not see it.

I said to Frida that I didn't know if I could stand it, the view so obvious day after day. There was nothing to miss or look forward to.

She laughed. 'People pay a fortune for the view to be so obvious.'

Frida lived some way back from the Esplanade, up a hill on one of the smaller side streets leading away from the water. It was a 1930s apartment building, white-painted brick with exposed polished half-bricks ornamentally punctuating the walls. The upper-floor apartments had balconies.

Her apartment—she pointed to it from the outside—was the one with a curved balcony and curved window at the western edge of the building. It got the afternoon sun, she said. We walked up two flights of stairs with thick, dark-green metal railings and smooth concrete steps. She put a key in the lock, turned it once and pushed the door open. You entered the living room first, the air dry and cool. It smelled of wood and coffee, and perhaps the sea. There was a familiarity in the smell, the air and light, as though I was returning to somewhere I'd known or wanted to be. There was one bedroom and a kitchen and bathroom. A long, low wooden coffee table in the middle of the living room had a few neat piles of books on it, a vase with dried baby's breath. On the wall, a few small sketches of beach scenes.

'I love it here,' I said.

'There,' she said, 'there—go onto the balcony.' She swept across the room ahead of me, a movement sure and graceful, and opened the balcony door. The wooden floorboards fanned in a herringbone pattern across the floor. There was something tidal about the repetition of the V-shaped design, a feeling of walking out to or back from the sea, as I walked to the curved window. Like she'd told me, the bay was out of sight, but I could smell salt from the open door.

'I've been cooped up since my last flare,' she said. 'The illness. And now I'm addicted to this air.' She waved and breathed in and laughed, and again moved across the floor, as I followed, to the small kitchen where she made tea.

Frida never said the name of her illness, *the illness*, but it was obvious to me that we had the same kind. We had the outward signs: joints swelling, stiff necks, rashes on our palms. I guessed that, like me, she did not abide easily by the names we get and give. We were bodies, first and foremost. A diagnosis, like metaphor, was essential for others—to explain how we felt and elicit a medical response or an attempt at empathy. But to each other, it was sufficient to be a body in pain and to know that about one another.

Our encounter then felt different to when we were in the pool, as though out of the water our bodies didn't know each other as well. The conversation was sparse but not forced or awkward. I considered that our bodies were aligned first and foremost. We understood the pool, and pain. These particular conditions enabled us to subvert certain expectations, of conversation mostly, and permit other threads of understanding to form between us. I had never known a friendship like it. Frida wore a light layer of make-up, faint perfume. A tabby cat, extremely thin, skulked in warily, paused a good distance away and stared at me, then at Frida, as if to ask what on earth had she done, who was this stranger. Frida told me the cat had been found in a plastic bag.

'I got her from a rescue organisation. She's always on the alert. If she senses me walking behind her, she hisses and growls and runs ahead. She can't stand to be followed, as though it's always a threat. She can only see the world this way, poor thing. Her body is so full of old memories of fear. You poor thing you.' She ran her palm over the cat's thin back. The cat arched her spine upwards, into Frida's touch.

'She looks peaceful now,' I said.

'Oh yes. She's slowly learned what comfort is and how to dwell in it. She lies in front of the gas heater all through the winter. It's as though, after all those long nights outside as a street cat, now she can't get enough of the warmth. But she will probably never truly trust me.'

Leading me back out into the living room, Frida pointed—'There'—as though she had just remembered the reason for inviting me. 'In the afternoons, the wall there is flooded with light and shadows. The shadows shake and run; sometimes they look like running water.' She put her fingers to her mouth and laughed once, surprised at herself. 'It's ridiculous but it can make me cry. It's just so simple.'

We watched the autumn glow against the wall, the shadows of leaves and clouds forming all kinds of impressions that dripped and glittered.

She asked, 'Do you drink wine? We should drink wine together.'

I was energised by everything she said. With Frida, there seemed time and capacity for everything. She took away the teacups and brought out two stemmed glasses, poured us each a measure of red wine, and we stood together on the balcony, breathing in the fresh air.

'Should we go to the Sea Baths?' asked Frida. 'It's not far.'

Back then spontaneity felt distant to me, a remembered feeling rather than something I was able to do. I thought that I wanted to go. 'I don't have my bathers.'

'Let's just walk and look. You can see it at least. I would love you to see it.'

She put the glasses in the sink, picked up her keys and bag, and made for the door, as though there was nothing more to think about. I hurried after her, a little light-headed.

We walked down the hill towards the water. Without speaking, Frida took my arm above the elbow, held on as the descent grew steeper. We reached the Esplanade and she let go. We crossed the road to where the Sea Baths faced the bay. Inside, two large pools glowed blue through fogged windows, a gym throbbed dully with music, the cafe was quiet. We passed through the building and reached the deck on the other side, leading down to the sand and the water.

—

We didn't swim that day. I realise now, knowing her captivation, her obsession with the water, that it was significant and singular, Frida allowing me this slow entry into her world and the water. We walked on the sand, put our feet in the chill shallows, drank coffee at the cafe.

I watched two women jog into the water and dive under the cold waves. 'I want to love this,' I told her. 'The air and the cold. I've been cooped up too, with the illness. The operation. I want my body to need this and make me want it.'

'Oh, but it does,' Frida said. Her voice had something sleek and loving about it. She also watched the women. 'The body—it will love it. You'll see. It already does.'

And with that lenient indoctrination into her habits, the water she loved, I was taken entirely into Frida's world.

I make no claims to singularity. In fact I've heard a story like this before. I sat outside an Italian cafe in Carlton, the one I visited often, the young waiters in white shirts milling about, espresso cups scattered on round concrete tables. At the table near me a woman spoke to her husband and another woman about a work colleague. She was trying to convey the strange likeness she felt between the woman and herself. She told them how even other colleagues at the office marvelled at the similarity between the women. It was true that they did look alike in some ways, she said; their height, the colour of their hair, the way they both tended to dress, *Like this, you know*, she gestured to her outfit: a black blazer, white shirt and tailored black trousers. But beyond that, the similarities were mostly internal, almost a way of being, of seeming to others, more so than a physical likeness. *People get us mixed up*. She said it as a point of pride. Her husband joked, *You've got a girl crush*. Her friend listened and nodded mildly. But the woman was insistent. Her husband and friend just didn't understand how it felt for her. She'd found someone, the woman repeated, who was just like her. *Even our manager says we remind her of each other, just in the way we are.* The woman's friend nodded more encouragingly, which seemed to compel her to reiterate with more urgency the feeling she was trying to convey. *It's just funny how often people say it and get us mixed up. It's made me feel strangely close to her, as if she's some long-lost twin.* She laughed. *She's just like me.* Her husband took a brisk sip of his espresso. Her friend looked around, as if waiting for someone. The conversation was over, and I later considered what the woman was asking for, or trying to express, as she told this to her husband and friend. I wondered what she was really saying with her story.

It was miraculous, the friendship, Frida and me. I would say it was sudden, a feeling of hurtling into good.

One day, after a hydrotherapy class, Frida suggested we meet to swim. *Swim properly*, she said.

It had been years since I had done this, been to a pool to swim, joined strangers in a lap lane, since I had pushed and pulled my body through water. When I took lessons as a child, and then through high school, it was nothing to swim up and back, up and back. All those lengths in a body I once knew.

She suggested the City Baths, in a red-brick Victorian building near the university. The entrance was reached by two identical staircases facing one another that rose up from street level. The main pool was much larger than the hydrotherapy pool, the thirty-metre expanse divided into six lanes. I thought again of how I gave up swimming lessons when I was fourteen, which seemed to me now like a first sin. Frida ducked under the lane rope and into the slow lane. She didn't look behind her, didn't look at me, only pushed off from the wall and started swimming. I followed her. My bad leg was slow; I kicked it without extending or flexing it fully, pulling myself along with my arms. I was swimming after all this time.

I made it to the other side and Frida was there, smiling.

'And then back,' she said, chest rising and falling.

Heart pounding, I followed her. I was slow. We repeated our laps and took a break, repeated this laps-and-break rhythm for ten minutes. It was all I could manage. Frida said I did well. I was good, she told me. *You did so good.* Her words were golden to me; I never spoke to myself like this. If I was alone, I wouldn't have swum half as many laps. It was all Frida, I knew this deeply. I was so certain about her.

From then on, we met to swim anywhere we could. We went to the City Baths, we met at hydrotherapy classes at the pool in Fitzroy, we met at the Carlton Baths outdoor pool—in a suburb surrounded by green: all the parks and the London plane trees on the walk from Parkville to Carlton, the pool flecked with gum leaves, the water turquoise and winking in the cool daylight. It became easier, each lap, I simply followed Frida. I just had to be like her, this was my steadfast belief. Our skin was parchment-dry after the pool. We stood near the steaming showers, quiet as we dried our limbs and torsos and feet. We coated our bodies in cold creams. Afterwards, we drank Italian coffee at the Carlton cafe with the wide terrazzo floors, where I'd heard the woman tell the story of her perceived double. Sparrows flitted about, landing on the chairs, on the tables, jumping to the floor, picking at scraps and crumbs.

We met in St Kilda to swim in the Sea Baths. We liked the water of the indoor pools, filled with warmed sea water, making the turquoise tiles gritty with sand. Sometimes I'd go to her apartment first and we would drink coffee standing on the balcony. Always standing, I stress this, as though poised to leave soon—underscoring that the pool was the actual destination and the coffee, the chatting, were mere preliminary acts.

We did not exchange phone numbers. We simply made a plan, a commitment and promise, to meet at one pool or another, and we would meet there. We were devout about the pool and our promises to each other.

If I aligned my body with Tomasz's in the early days, when we first met, I had now begun to orientate it by Frida's. We swam together, drank coffee together, ate together after our swims. I was convinced this was a path to betterment. The state of my body would be improved. We did not deal in cures, Frida and I. We did not seek healing. We sought betterment in the ways our bodies could be made better. I sought a narrative we might craft together, Frida and I, beyond mere dichotomies of sick and healthy, illness and wellness. I told her: 'I hate the talk of cures.'

She agreed. 'What we hate is the narrative of a cure. It's taken so long for us to accept that this miracle isn't possible for us. Then some well-meaning person tells you to take celery extract in tablet form and you'll be *as good as new*—is it actually well-meaning or just their assumption that I haven't tried hard enough, that I somehow missed this one extraordinary trick? I'm not looking for a cure—and what is this *new* they wish so much for me?—but for coexistence, some bearable accord between the illness and myself.'

We drank our coffee in the same way, a shot splashed with water. We breathed out the same bitter coffee breath, our teeth straight and slightly stained.

'You seem good,' said Tomasz. We were sitting at a Thai restaurant in North Melbourne. Perhaps he meant, *You seem happy.*

My elated chest and calm scalp. I couldn't convey it to him. 'I saw Frida today, the woman from the pool.'

I tried to describe for Tomasz the similarities, the soul-layer compatibility, as I saw it, how we were almost beyond words, Frida and I. The way our bodies seemed to act in parallel, identical ways. Our bodies seemed to have the same effect on us and who we felt ourselves to be, an affinity or likeness born of identical pains. A little of my excitement drained in the telling—it is always like this. I thought again of the woman in the Carlton cafe, talking about her double. Now here I was, making the same attempt at the impossible.

Tomasz did not know my body when it was well. Was I another person, then? If that was true, then he didn't know the other me, who had the body before. By this I mean before pain. He had sometimes asked, when I was difficult to be with, nagging and anxious, whether I felt I really had anybody to talk to aside from him. It was a legitimate question: to others I cultivated an impression I was loath to dismantle. I told people about my pain as though in a constant aftermath, hidden in the past tense (*I wasn't well yesterday, last week, last night*) or the vaguer and unfinished present perfect continuous (*My knees have been sore lately, I haven't been feeling well lately*), or I merely called in sick so as not to show others my worst days. It was difficult to explain to him that this cultivation of an appearance actually contributed to a feeling of wellbeing, of strength; that the figurative wall I manufactured was in fact protective, an enormous and structural talisman.

'She understands,' I said. 'No, it's not even that. She just knows. It's like she's me but not me.'

He took my hand in his, rubbed his thumb over my thumbnail. 'That's good.'

Harder still to explain that this attempt to display understanding in fact felt like a step away.

We began to live in a beautiful pattern, me and Frida: meet and swim, swim and be together. Frida always wanted to move.

'I have been like this forever,' she said. 'It's the way I'm meant to be.'

When her body first showed signs of the disease, Frida said, she'd hoped to work with it, as though the illness was some feral animal she could tame through hard work and diligence. And so she exercised her body far more than she once had—she emphasised she'd never been an athlete, had never been a *sportsperson*, this was purely a personal compulsion—and she found that this made her feel better. Not cured, not fixed of disease, but rather the strongest possible version of herself, measured against only herself, and this realisation that she had even an ounce of control over her body was addictive. There was a lightness in her. Her joints felt lighter. And so she kept it up, kept at it aggressively—that word she used.

She said she usually hated talking about it all, the disease, the body. As though words, once they left our mouths, exited the very thing that held the truth. With you it's different, she said. I was made giddy by her compliments.

She talked about the ideal time, the peak between body and self. She sought it, that point of equilibrium signified by a levity in her chest, a smooth static on the very edge of her skin.

'It's telling me I'm *here*,' she said. 'My mind finally reckons with it: I know I'm here in this body.'

She loved the cold water, she loved the movement. The feeling that the border between body and air was as thin as could be. Like stepping out into a cold night, the air meets you, you meet the air.

'I get excited,' said Frida, 'as if I have a thousand beginnings. Everything good is ahead of me.'

Frida wanted to do everything, I wanted to do everything, we wanted to do everything together. *I feel good*, I said to her. *I feel good*, she said. We felt good, we were together, and we were good together.

In the mornings we sometimes felt miraculous. We felt alive and our joints moved almost with ease. It's better when you don't think too much, said Frida. Just be your body moving through a room. *Just be your body*. What a radical statement to me, who had for years since the diagnosis resented the vessel I moved with and inside of, seemingly bound to it against my will.

After plunging into the saltwater pools in St Kilda, where we moved back and forth between the lap pool and the hydrotherapy spa, we stood outside and let the ocean gust overwhelm us. We closed our eyes and smiled. Our hair smelling of salt and threaded with cold. With Frida was happiness. I was the body when I was with her. I was more of my body. I was most content when I was moving. I thought I was most at peace with her. I was the person I liked the most, liked better, with her. Heartbeat strong and steady. We drank wine after swimming for an hour or more. The wine didn't make us sick. No nauseous, dry nights. Together, we were miraculous. I wondered if we were healing, if she was healing me. I made a point of going every day to the pool. I didn't care if it was possibly unsustainable. I attached myself to her, to this compulsion that carried us both out somewhere, out to sea.

It was good with Frida; I was good with her. When I got home from the pool, Tomasz would say, *You're so happy today.* I moved lightly. *It's Frida*, I'd say. *We're happy together.*

This is the way you know your own body: the fleshy rise of the stomach; the scars you remember getting and those you don't; the places where the hair grows more and thicker—the line from genitals to navel, the single hair through a mole; the places that hurt today or always; the deep line under one eye; the parts you see first in every mirror. It is the buried heavy knowledge of a sister's body you've grown with, a best friend's you live with and eventually bleed in sync with. In Frida's presence I had come back to it, arrived back inside my body, reacquainted with what I'd estranged myself from.

I went back to the surgeon's rooms in the converted, affluent-looking brick house in Richmond. A home once, now a place for tending to bones. Hips, knees, and spines. Floorboards now for crutches and expensive specialists' shoes. A water fountain and a television blaring a Channel 9 talk show like a warped technicolour children's program inadvertently broadcast to adults. I always tried to read while waiting. When he called me in for my appointment, I walked in with cautious confidence. I let myself indulge in the gore of me that he had seen: the scalpel across my pelvis, sawing off my bone and throwing it away. Strange that this neat and contained and faintly greying yet youthful man had seen this. He said, *You seem well*, and I said, *I feel good*. I thought of telling him about Frida, how I had met another body like mine. I imagined him saying, *This is no cure, no person can fix you*. And I knew that I didn't want to hear this. I imagined him saying, *You feel good because you are recovering, because you've had the major operation you needed*—and although that may have been true, I also did not want to hear this. It was Frida. I lay on the bed while he held my left leg and moved it this way and that, manipulating the hip joint into new directions that released a sudden, all-skin all-mind fear across my body. *It's okay*, he said, and I wondered if I'd gasped. *It's moving well. You're doing so well.* He released my leg and I let my breath go. *I'm swimming lots, too*, I said. *Good*, he said. And I resisted any words about Frida, lest I seem idealistic or naive. Yet I felt her there with me, as the surgeon congratulated me on how well I was doing and moving and progressing. Frida was there. As I walked down the smooth concrete steps of the former house, out into the light and careless breeze, she was there.

Frida, Frida, Frida. It was good with Frida. I was good with her, I was sure of this.

Once mid-April and the cold arrived, in the changing rooms of Melbourne's public swimming pools I'd hear people ask, *Where do you go in winter?* As in, what water do you find? *I don't like the City Baths,* some would say. *Too crowded, too stuffy.* Others: *Kensington, maybe. It was easier when I lived south side; there's Brighton Baths, there's the sea.* I liked to listen to them talk; sometimes I even nodded and joined in. I liked the gentle energy of the changing room, the others talking about their days or their pains or their partners, with an openness matching our naked bodies that seemed different from conversations outside. A woman whose daughter had just miscarried, another who had left her husband of forty years. The many languages of this country ringing in the chlorinated air. And now here I was, part of it.

Nobody wanted the outdoor suburban pools to close. Nobody wanted to go inside. The pools in Carlton and North Melbourne were heated until the end of April, until the first cold mornings, until my mother would report the first frosts from my hometown. They would close for the winter and early spring, and reopen in October.

This day I remember: we met to swim at the Carlton Baths. Frida was waiting for me. Certainly it was colder in the air. The heated outdoor pool, enclosed by a high brick wall, steamed in the morning air. A white diaphanous mist hovered above the water and my feet ached with the cold. It was beautiful: the cold, the ache, the stark reality of it. After all those good days—a sense of levity, distance from the operation and the hospital—a familiar, cloudy feeling of pain had returned. It may have been caused by the first truly cold day of the season. Or that may be too simplistic an explanation. But it is so akin to weather, the sometimes-bewildering transformations, the oscillation and unpredictability of a body, the following, inexorable quality of familiar pain.

There was only one other person in the pool, a man confidently moving his body up and down the fast lane. His arms arced through the white morning steam. Frida and I each took a lane and swam parallel to one another. We rested at the shallow end; we rarely talked. I was more tired than usual. Frida swam much faster than me. Tomasz, the physiotherapist, and my sister who was a nurse had told me to be careful. This new friend of yours has not just had the same operation as you, they said. She isn't in recovery like you are. I wanted to say: *But look at us! She is so like my body, I am so like her body, we can do the same things. We swim together. We are miraculous when we swim together.* I wanted to say this to them all.

That day, I worried I was not keeping up with Frida, with her body. The man in the fast lane intimidated me, though he didn't so much as glance in our direction. I tried not to think, to focus only on the body, and kept swimming. It felt good, for a time; I felt good. Frida and I swam and swam and I was sure we felt good together, side by side. I kept telling myself this. Frida knew it too.

When we got out of the pool, I was unsteady. Freezing in the cold morning air. Frida loved it and I wanted to smile with her, but I was sure there were people around, perhaps looking through the windows of the gym, observing the way I walked, with the limp I'd never quite lost, and seeing that my knees, my hurting knees, didn't bend properly and were unbalanced, awkward. That's why I'm slow today, I said to myself. It's my knees, my bad knees. Swollen skin encasing hot stone. And my neck, that's why I'm slow today; my neck grips my spine, sends this taut pain over my scalp and ear and right eye.

'You're okay,' said Frida.

'How do you know?'

'Just be in your body.' She had said something similar before.

'I'm okay.' I agreed with her, tried to think just like her.

'Just be in your body in this place.'

There were days when I didn't swim. This is obvious, but they were significant to me. On the days when I didn't swim, I felt less definition in the world. I barely escaped a feeling of failure.

On the days when I didn't swim, I walked. I walked mostly in Royal Park. We lived close to that park and the three hospitals nearby: the Women's, the Children's, the Royal Melbourne. Connecting parklands surrounded the buildings, forming a green mass north of the city. A tram line ran from the city and along past the hospitals with a stop for each, through the park, past the zoo and into the suburbs, to Brunswick and Coburg. One newer area of the park, with a playground and paths, stood on the site of the old Children's hospital. A steep, grassy hill looked out over the playground towards the city. Further north along the paths were patches of what signs called *remnant vegetation* and a circle of native grasses hemmed in by a bitumen path. Dogs were allowed to run off the leash in that section. The colossal thick eucalypts and golden-wattle acacia trees, the kangaroo grass and soft spear grass bowing in the wind, made it unlike Melbourne's other, heavily Europeanised, colonised parks.

On a quiet day, if you caught a snatch of sound devoid of traffic from the nearby arterial roads, heard only insect hum and a bellbird with its sweet, spiky call, saw only the sight of the gums and grasses, the colours of brown and straw and bottle green, you might be transported out of the city and into far-off national parks that preserved by decree what was once the entire landscape.

It had rained recently, nearing the end of April, the deepening of autumn, and the dogs ran across the circle and threw themselves in the muddy water of miniature lakes. On all the other paths and green spaces in the rest of the parkland, the dogs had to be leashed, under the control of their owners. I loved to watch them run ecstatically, released, though it terrified me when they came too close.

You always walk in the same places, Tomasz would say to me. If we walked together, he always sought a new path, a new way home, a road we weren't absolutely sure would lead where we hoped it would. A sense of the new and unknown excited him. I didn't like this, especially when my neck and skull ached, when my knees hurt. Impatient, I would say, *Let's just go this way. I know this way.* Depending on many things—the sky, the day, my neck, my legs—I would either insist resolutely on the way home I knew, or relent—*Fine, let's go your way*—and let him find a new way home. It was probably never as bad as I anticipated, that unknown path, the outcome of taking it so dependent on variables we couldn't possibly predict. I knew my little essential habits made me seem unspontaneous, were perhaps unintelligible to him. The seeking of safety was difficult to convey.

I tried to walk a certain distance in the quieter times of day. I still couldn't walk far without the leg tiring, and when it did I knew that I was limping again, as though I had gone back in time, occupying the body I had before the surgery. I hated this. As if there had been no healing or betterment at all. Royal Park was crowded on the weekends, full of families with bikes and scooters, young and fit running groups sculpted in lycra and polyester, couples in beanies and leggings walking greyhounds and whippets, and, closer to the Children's hospital, sometimes a young patient in a wheelchair and beside them a parent or nurse, taking in the air and sunlight, the child with an IV in their arm or oxygen prongs in their nose, wheeled through a park and playground they could view but not entirely participate in.

Before I left the house, I stood on the balcony and crushed paracetamol with my back teeth. Two tablets at a time, six tablets per day.

At that time it calmed me, to rely on that small dose of painkillers. When I was first unwell, I'd rarely take even a single pill. As a graduate student in England, where I lived for a year when I was twenty-four, my body was fragile and inflamed. A college friend, an English guy, once said to me: *If there is a pill to fix any problem with me, I will take it.* He studied politics and philosophy and enjoyed arguing about hypothetical, conceptual questions. I told him I didn't agree. A pill numbed, I said, it didn't fix the cause. In the college dining hall we debated, in a benign way we both enjoyed, and I was unusually confident about what I was saying. He believed wholeheartedly in a pill to fix it all. I shook my head. Such thinking was, I said, like discarding our rubbish in a bin to be hauled away; while it was no longer in our sight, the rubbish would nevertheless exist forever. Surely there was something, some truth to be learned, that would be lost in that absolute numbing he sought. It wasn't that I believed pain to be wholly good or bad, but my friend's pursuit of its total absence seemed to signify a refusal to understand pain. He didn't want to mine and unearth its causes when to do so might have fixed greater or underlying ills. It was as though I believed my pain was saying something other than asserting its pure existence, and to constantly silence even the most feeble utterance would be to ignore more urgent and lasting messages.

On rare occasions, when I lived on the cobblestone street adjoining the college and plunged into isolating cycles of pain, while around me the people I studied with ran laps of Christ Church meadow and rowed the River Cherwell and played football in University Parks, I gave in and took a pill. Often just one tablet. I would sweat through the night, my body shocked at the relief, listening to the dregs of parties ebb down the street and in the gardens of adjacent colleges. Along the way something shifted. It wasn't that the pain worsened and I acquiesced. Rather, something loosened a little in my staunch beliefs—though perhaps that loosening was precisely because of cumulative or worsening pain—and I let myself take a more regular dose. Now it seems near impossible to retrace and explain the memory of pain and the thoughts I had at those times.

And so years later, in the early months after the surgery, I kept crushing the tablets with my teeth, three times a day.

I was walking in Royal Park one morning. I left early while Tomasz slept. I knew I would not swim that day and I had not swum the day before, nor the day before that. I'd been nauseous in the night and first thing in the morning, as though I'd eaten too much or too much of something. I worried that I wouldn't ever go again to the pool, wouldn't see Frida and swim with her. It was so easy, and so hard, not to go. Once I decided that I wouldn't swim that day (*I won't swim today, I'm not going*) the relief was immense. The guilt was immense. I knew that if I took my body into the water, I would feel good. My legs would feel good. My bad leg would get stronger. I would see Frida and she would swim too, and we'd be good together. But my thoughts were leaden that day and through the days before it, and strong: they had such power over anything my body might have needed or wanted. They were cumbersome, torpid, material; they were as heavy as my knees were, as heavy as the concrete, burning, arthritic feeling that had planted itself in me and which meant I didn't want to swim, or which was caused by my failure to swim—a point of difference I couldn't easily distinguish—that sent me frantic even in my lethargy. While Tomasz was busy at work or in his workshop on the weekends, making things and noise, I only wanted to sit and breathe and be still. I was annoyed when Tomasz or anyone tried to excuse it. *You're still recovering. It's early days.* None of this consoled me. I convinced myself that I must walk.

I walked to the hill in the park closest to the Children's hospital. From one side it looked out over the playground, towards the city. From the other it faced the hospital and parklands and the circle of native grasses. People sat up on the hill to watch sunsets in the summer, with cider or ice cream, or ran up and down it in running shorts and shoes, replicating great struggles. Children and dogs ran over the crest of the hill; occasionally a toddler tumbled partway down like a ragdoll. That morning the hill was deserted and I walked up it without an audience, and because of that absence it didn't seem so steep.

Industrial smoke bred with real clouds over the city buildings. The city was as though under water, a salvaged Atlantis emerging green, grey, and blue. It was seven in the morning and the smog-cloud creations resembled sand drifts sent up by the tails of fish. I became absorbed in an image of the grassy hill I stood on having been formed after the old Children's hospital was demolished, moulded by the buried things underneath it: a grave of X-ray machines, a thousand pairs of doctor's gloves.

A large flock of galahs populated the surroundings. Their pink-and-grey feathers, their high screeching, stood out in what was really a city landscape. On the footpaths, the park designers had imprinted bird claw prints on the concrete, to give the appearance of nature. Some parts of the park, closest to the hospitals, were full of the false green of introduced European grasses, meeting the concrete paths which led to the new, many-windowed buildings. There was a designated wetland, further towards Flemington, indicating the natural origins of the land, before water was buried by city and road, as well as an ornamental pond on the Parkville edge, fed by stormwater and populated by ducks and egrets and clouds of mosquitoes in summer.

In the park I saw the same people often. I wondered whether, like me, they avoided the nine am weekend morning peak, the friends who walked two or three abreast, and the weekday late afternoon rush, the after-work athletes; the fast ones, the fit ones, the ones who ran with dogs. I knew that I still walked with a kind of lilting gait and I had stopped, or tried to stop, thinking about its conspicuousness.

  I saw a man I'd seen before, in his early forties, with those strange soft shoes that look like gloves. He winced as he walked, a visible and rhythmic fissure in his facial expression, there and then not and then there again. We said or nodded hello, or sometimes one or both of us avoided eye contact. There was the well-known white artist who lived in North Melbourne, with long, curly, greying hair and a thick and wafting biblical beard, who ran through the parks and the suburbs regularly. His loose shorts sat high on his hamstrings, his legs muscular and firm with a coating of wiry hair, and I jealously regarded his bodily strength as an ingredient of his art.

I saw a woman who often sat on a bench seat near the Children's hospital. Since the operation I had seen her several times, always on what appeared to be my bad days. Nurses and support care workers, administrative and cafe workers, often sat on the seats there. They might have an early cigarette before work, or sit down on their lunch breaks. The relatives of patients came there too, with their bright pink VISITOR stickers named and dated on their chests.

I had noticed the woman before, in the early mornings, perhaps because of certain similarities. She was, I guessed, around thirty years old and had auburn-blonde hair like mine, a stiff sort of posture that suggested discomfort, yet nevertheless a quiet confidence about her. She sat with one leg crossed over the other, and she sat very still. I joined her on the bench that morning when I wasn't going to the pool and when I hadn't been there for days and didn't know when

I would swim again. I crossed my good leg over the other. As I tend to do when I meet someone who brings about in me an odd sense of recognition, I wondered if she was in pain. Her hands were hidden inside gloves, her body in a thick, baggy green jumper. Along with a sense of alertness there was a guardedness in the way she held herself.

We sat next to each other, the woman and me, surrounded by the park, surrounded by the hospitals.

'I've seen you here before,' she said. 'I'm Sylvia.'

'I've seen you here, too.'

'How is your leg?' she asked, as if continuing a conversation we'd had yesterday.

I told her that I'd had an operation less than eight weeks ago.

'This is the so-called recovery time,' I said. 'I'm told to take it slow. I'm not working for a while yet. I don't really need to be anywhere.'

'I understand.' Sylvia nodded and raised her shoulders and pulled her woollen sleeves further over her hands in what seemed to me to be an act of protection. She looked squarely at me; she had large brown eyes. 'I feel like I recognise you,' she said, 'from sometime so long ago.'

I told her I felt the same.

And so Sylvia entered my life, though we were such likenesses of one another, something internally similar, that she was already familiar to me. Sylvia—meaning my conception of her, the Sylvia I knew—might have always been present in my life. This may mean only that the person I was in front of Sylvia had always been there, and was therefore familiar. These people who enable the truest expression of ourselves are rare. Maybe we don't know a person all that well, but in the mirror of them we know ourselves. I'd begun to think I should like to find them all, these other ones, my doubled and tripled and multiplied versions, my internal mirrors.

'I seem to just want to sit today,' I said to her, as though it were an inexplicable or unforgivable admission. 'I want to sit and yet I want to swim in the ocean and be freezing and good.' I noticed that my voice shook. Unwonted, for me especially, was the near-collapse that seemed imminent when I was around this woman I didn't even know. As though I might lie in her lap and weep and she would soothe me like my mother did. Where was the self-possessed resilience I prided myself on presenting to Tomasz, to the doctor, to my parents, even to Frida?

'You don't need the ocean today,' said Sylvia. Her voice was sweet and deep. I thought of the darkest honey. 'You can just sit today. We can just sit today. It's okay. We're in pain.'

She slowly shifted her crossed leg down, and crossed the other over it. 'Tell me about the hospital.'

Behind us stood the enormous, towering hospital, the one for children. We didn't look at it. Sylvia touched her fingers, her knuckles, through the woollen layer of her gloves. Unaccountably, I had the sense that even if her body was incredibly compromised, as I guessed it was, nothing would quite transgress upon who she was, her beliefs and their expression. A combination of vulnerability and staunchness, that is what I noticed about her.

    I told her: I was in the hospital for five days. Convalescence, the rise-and-fall of the word, like a day, like breathing. I surprised myself, still, by how much it comforted me: the enclosure, the regular meals, being cared for through nights, the nurses with their alternating comforting or stern manners, the views over the concrete heights, views of over there and anywhere I wasn't. The watching of the outside, never threatened by any sky. There was freedom in all that control, it was what might be asked of childhood.

Was it a cliché to talk about the lack of darkness, the eternal persistent fluorescence of a hospital? The wide, lit hallways at night, the lulling light touching the edges of the bed. As a child I liked to think of the countries where it wasn't nighttime, so that I was not the only one in the world who was awake in the dark. In the wild, deep isolation that seems possible in childhood, I thought I was the only one not sleeping in my hemisphere of the world. In the hospital you will always find someone awake, if you need it, if you need to know it.

And convalescence, the oceanic rise-fall of the word, a chest breathing, recovery. I saw a flushed sunrise over Richmond through a top-floor window. A shared room is to hear the night sounds of others, when we are calling—for nurses, water, painkillers, mothers. There was a young nurse. For two days I had not stood up but rather lay like a cut-down statue, rigid and breathing. The pain that comes from this immobility is one of longing, a need for movement; painkilling tablets cannot penetrate it. The young nurse came to me, I was sighing and stirring like an infant. She said something to me in a three am whisper, took my body in her hands and rolled me on my side. She squeezed a thick cold cream into one hand and she massaged it across my bad leg, up and down the thigh. As the blood began to move through my leg I felt such relief, I couldn't really communicate it. I could've cried. She knew that sometimes what the body demands with its pain is not pills but another body, is care.

As I confessed all this to Sylvia I noted, somewhere in the back of my mind, that I hadn't told Tomasz this story and hadn't in fact told it to anyone else.

And I told Sylvia how, as soon as I was home, I missed it: the hospital and its routine, the safety of its control. At home, released into apparent freefall, a stark, real space akin to surfacing above water to the crowded reality of a summer pool, I could not be okay anywhere; not in the bedroom of our share house with the steep staircase, not with Tomasz and the edges of our relationship, or in the small lounge room downstairs where I went occasionally if the nurse or my parents were visiting and which I reached after a feat, grasping crutches and Tomasz holding me as if I were a drunkard. The unpredictability of life outside the hospital was wild to me. I cried once, at the splitting open.

I told all this to the woman named Sylvia. We sat side by side on the bench in the park, the hospital behind us, looming and quiet, always full of people and light. A winding path cut through the neat grass into the playground.

'As children,' said Sylvia, 'we get sick, we take our first day off from school, we have a cold, a sore throat, we are tired, we vomit. How do we feel about that day? Are we sad or guilty or angry for all that we are missing out on, to be away from our friends, to have exited our small world for the day? Or are we relieved, secretly, to be able to hide away?' She looked ahead, towards the eucalypt treetops and the city beyond.

I was one of the relieved ones, Sylvia told me in a voice almost conspiratorial, low and smiling. The sky ahead was grey, splintering in pieces to gold, to blue. She liked to be home, once the initial guilt of failing to be where she should be had passed. There was a wonderful absolution from responsibility. Once it had been decided that she would stay home, when she told her mother she felt sick and her mother agreed, yes, you should stay home, and had called the school to tell them, *Sylvia isn't coming in today*, the relief was dizzying. *Sylvia will not be there; she is staying home.* She realised that the things she thought were important—that lesson, that assignment or activity—were not as critical as she'd believed. Not in the sense that she could refuse to do them if she were at school, but that in her absence those things went on without her. Her teachers, her friends, her homework, her class job to clean this or that—in other words, the order she lived by, the requirement to be at school for a certain time every day and to leave it and then return the next day—did not need her. The world did not actually need her.

Perhaps, Sylvia suggested, the way we felt about that first sick day determined our relationship with sickness in the years to come. The sofa and a blanket, butter-menthol lollies for a sore throat, the daytime television shows, and her mother—who, she told Sylvia years later, was secretly relieved when one of them, Sylvia or her sisters, stayed home. She missed them when they left for school, despite any stress of rearranging a work shift or taking a day of leave. The sick day, at its most benign, offers the ability to act out a longing to return to seclusion, mother and child alone together, the precious time when we are allowed to shut out the world. We turn inwards in what might be a primal act of protection. We don't need to go anywhere. We are advised not to go outside. She spoke of the sick day with something bordering on reverence.

'And there is no shame in this,' Sylvia said. 'I believe this.'

I told her that those states of allowance, forgiveness, or exemption had blurred for me such that I didn't know if I was living the equivalent of a protracted sick day or was in recovery, and when either state would end. I wondered whether I was still allowed to be removed from life and at what point I was unnecessarily fused to my excuses. There was a confusion of condition, in the case of chronic illness.

I explained that I was a postgraduate student, in my final year, and had taken sick leave for twelve weeks, though I worried that amount of time was excessive, especially as some of it was unpaid. I had stopped tutoring for a semester, stopped the one day a week of office work, the purely mechanical editing work, that I'd done for the previous year. I didn't feel relaxed. I felt guilty and severed from some essence that was being denied me.

'Perhaps the thing denied to you is a real sick day,' said Sylvia. 'When it's permitted to not be okay, to be healing, cared for, to not need to go outside.'

Even if this were true, when I was demonstrably well, when I was out in what we called the world, I felt, because of the potential of the illness, its quiet, slow-burn ruination, separate yet again. I didn't tell her about Frida, about the pool or all those good days, the ones that seemed now to be phantoms.

Sylvia offered to walk me home. I said that I lived close by. She could visit me sometimes, if she wanted. We could sit outside on the balcony. I felt a certainty in our encounter, that we were now joined in a way not easily broken. That we were already truthful to each other.

'A balcony is the perfect place,' she said. 'You are outside without the pressures of being outside. You are outside with the safety of being inside.'

I smiled at her.

We started to walk home. We were surrounded by the park, surrounded by the hospitals.

'You're anxious,' she said. 'The walking.'

'Yes,' I said, 'I am. I'm anxious. The walking. It's all so different after the operation. Aren't you, too? Aren't you anxious?'

'I am,' she said. 'I am. But you will get home.' She took my arm, hooking her elbow in mine. It was not clear who was helping the other to walk.

I told her, I know this; I told her, I have to get home. I am just anxious about it, I said, the walking; the walking is so different now. I found it difficult then: anger was a half-step away from the anxiety, anger was inextricable from my very steps. I didn't want to get angry at this new friend I'd only just met, who was very familiar to me. I was so drawn inwards by the hurting, equivalent to a fear of movement, it was hard to tell if I had spoken aloud or just to myself.

'It's my leg, my thigh,' I said.

'If you name the place, does it make a difference?' she asked.

'Of course not.'

'Of course it does.'

And on like this. She walked me home. Sylvia walked me home. This was Sylvia. My firm yet kind Sylvia. In naming, we overcome silence. She said this and other strange and poetic things that might have been close to my thoughts, and I loved her for this.

After this encounter I felt calmer. I forgave myself for not swimming. When Tomasz came home and asked innocently, *Did you swim today?* I thought instead of Sylvia, and as though putting on the persona of that other woman, stepping inside her skin, I said, *No, I didn't swim today. I just need to rest at the moment.* Tomasz didn't seem to notice anything different in what I'd said or the way I said it, but in truth I couldn't believe I could utter this and even more so that I could abide it. It's hard to convey how little I valued rest, how much I judged it as a vice and, in my lowest moments, an iniquity.

Though the Parkville terrace house was cold in the autumn mornings, the balcony was often saturated with sun. After midday it passed over the house, the light gone until the following day. I put coffee on the stovetop as Sylvia stood in the dim kitchen. She had just arrived, her first visit. On the day we met she had walked me home from the park, stood at the doorway and told me to go in, sit down, lie down—*just rest*, she said—and then she left.

Sylvia encouraged rest. I would say she was devout about it. On the day of her visit I hadn't wanted to go to the pool, I didn't even want to walk around Royal Park. I hadn't done the long walk I'd made a sort of promise to myself to do, around the circle of native grasses, over to the zoo, tracing its fenced perimeter, from where I'd sometimes hear the improbable low growl of a lion, a burst of elephant noise, children's animated cries, up the hill and back to the park. I hadn't done this and felt miserable about it, guilty and accountable, it seemed, for any ills my body experienced afterwards. With Sylvia, permission was granted. This was clear from who she was, how she was. We were allowed to be still. I was allowed to go nowhere.

In the kitchen that morning, Sylvia stood very still, hands in her pockets, shivering slightly. Her lips were blue at the edges, and the low light paled her skin. I felt such affection for her, even though I didn't know her well at all. I understood her pain with an arresting kind of certainty, not unlike the way I'd been on first witnessing Frida make her way out of the pool. I poured the coffees, added hot water to each. We walked up the stairs.

The Victorian terrace house was old. People gasped when they saw the steep stairwell, shook their heads in disbelief after their first trip up and down, to use the bathroom or see the view from our balcony, aghast at how we could— how could I, what with my knees, *your knees, how do you do it?*—walk up and down them every day. Tomasz always ran down the stairs, hurtling, fast. I called him the hurricane as he tore down to the ground floor, I laughed when I said it: *It's coming, Hurricane Tomasz.* I was used to the stairs. I even told people, as though trying to prove a moral argument, that it was good for me, for my knees to bend and strengthen. It's good for me, I insisted.

This was often my response to those who spoke about rest, who told me that certain actions were impossible or ill-advised for me, that I should *take it easy*, that I needed to learn to be idle, restore energy, care for myself and my body. In response I would say that if I didn't move, I would become a statue. Stone, marble, immovable. The idea of rest, of pure stopping, the attendant fragility I perceived, was abhorrent to me, a sign of failure and weakness and giving into the illness. Until I met Sylvia.

We sat on the balcony. The sun on our faces, our heads. Sylvia wore a thick woollen jumper, deep emerald green, and brought the cuffs to the tips of her red-painted fingernails. Soft edges, steam from our coffee cups. We felt warm, contented.

There was nowhere to go. My eyelids were heavy with sunlight. A faint shock at this unpressured moment.

'This old thing was my grandma's,' she said, lifting her arms. The thick sleeves of emerald wool hung loosely from her hidden hands. 'She grew up dead poor and was obsessed with quality.'

'My grandmother, my father's mother, she had soft woollen cardigans, large and loose, navy with gold buttons,' I said. 'I can smell them now that you make me think of them.'

Sylvia brought an elbow to her nose, sniffed and smiled. 'Same. We are the same. I remember the perfume—but it's gone now, of course.' She had large straight teeth and full lips. Her nose was long with a middle ridge, a bump, more noticeable from the side. Her features reminded me of me.

'They're all dead now,' said Sylvia. 'It's amazing to me just how absent they are. The houses they lived in have either been demolished, become townhouses or been renovated by strangers. The most intimate things—their pyjamas, his shaver and soap, her purse, her hairbrush—all disappear. And now it's just us left. Just our bodies.'

I told Sylvia how sometimes I thought my body was made up of all of them: their poor diets, insomnias, anxieties, their traumas. These grandparents who had known poverty and violence and migration. The body historical. Otherwise it was hard to explain the swiftness with which the disease had taken me. Or was that too easy a formulation, too lazy an attempt to trace the cause?

'Maybe, or perhaps not. Either way, it's the only body you can be in,' said Sylvia. She drank her coffee in a few deep sips.

The body is historical. It can only be this way. We find ourselves there. You could say that I exist in a depiction of *The Temptation of St. Anthony*, painter unknown, fifteenth or maybe sixteenth century, Flemish or Dutch. Renaissance disease. I recognise myself. The beggar in the left-hand corner: his hand is bent at a right angle, the wrist bone looks swollen, as does the knuckle of the index finger. His face looks aghast at this, his world.

The body historical. These limbs, cheekbones, eyelids, forehead of creased centuries; we are identical, we are never really new. Bodies, bodies more. And we exist, Frida and Sylvia and I, in *The Three Graces* by Peter Paul Rubens. Of the three, thought to signify beauty, creativity, and fertility, the woman on the left, the first grace, if you look at it that way, has a disfigured left hand, half bent, hyperextended, and possibly a swollen knee. The finger joints fold in like the deep waves of skin become old. It is thought that, depending on your impression, this is evidence of either a clumsy painting technique or of an illness that was appearing with more frequency in the seventeenth century. A much older painting by Rubens, *The Miracles of Saint Ignatius Loyola*, from 1618, shows what is sometimes called the *swan's neck* deformity of the hands from rheumatoid arthritis. According to contemporary sources, Rubens suffered from this disease, and painted his own hands in his paintings, transposing them onto people of any gender, thereby representing his body through that of another figure. Some suggest that the bulged, misshapen hands acted almost as a kind of signature in his paintings. It is thought that, if a scan of his finger joints could be performed, then a more definitive post-death diagnosis could be made, but Rubens' bones have been lost to history.

The disease is well-documented, however, in the case of Pierre-Auguste Renoir. There are many black-and-white photographs, and one short video, of the painter in his wheelchair, strips of cloth wrapped around his hands, thought to help him hold his brush but more likely to prevent the nails of his bent fingers tearing the flesh of his palms. From this chair he continued to paint, creating his lasting identity in renditions of halcyon summer picnics; soft summer grasses, fields of wildflower, doll-like faces, long white dresses and boating and nostalgia.

And the other, bodily paintings I think of: Frida Kahlo in the plaster corsets that encased her body after the accident on a bus with her boyfriend when she was eighteen, her pelvis pierced by a metal handrail. In what sounds like an ingredient of metaphor, a fantastic literary detail, a man who stood near her on the bus that day carried a bag of gold powder. It burst on impact, showering Frida's injured body with gold. Blood, gold, and bone.

Frida painted the corsets she was compelled to wear, lying in the bed to which she was often confined, a mirror positioned so that she could paint either self-portraits or her corset-encased body, which was perhaps the same thing. I picture her, statuesque, in plaster. She wore these corsets often throughout her life, a necessary support for her spine. She became the work; her body wore it. Frida's body was always the first work.

Sylvia visited again a few days later. I made coffee on the stovetop while she stood there, looking cold. This time Sylvia wore black leggings and a woollen turtleneck jumper, ruby red, her hands and neck buried as always. Hair tied back in a high bun, like a ballet dancer. Her neck was stiff; she could barely move her head. When she turned to me, she turned her shoulders, her whole body, not unlike a statue that can only be shifted on its plinth.

'How is your leg today?'

'How is your neck today?'

'I'm looking for the words,' said Sylvia. 'I have them and I don't have them. Doctors like numbers. *How is your pain? On a scale of one to ten? Give me a number.* I grew obsessed with these numbers, once. I was obsessed. I'd try to name my morning. *Today is a three. Today is a nine.* I'd name my evenings and my nights, eight, nine, ten. Up-down-up-up-down. When can you ever really say, *Today is a ten?* Does that mean you have hit the limit of what you can take? Does it mean you cannot go any higher? And if you say eleven, is that saying you refuse to take any more, or that you've kicked over this linguistic house of cards, you refuse to go by this constructed numbers game?' She gave a brief, breezy laugh and waved a hand in the air.

We went to the balcony. The ginkgos on the footpath, full and yellow, bounced lightly, and beyond them the plane trees across the street shuddered. It was easy to sit and watch them.

I told Sylvia about what I called my silly dream.

'A while ago, I had this dream about running. I had it again last night, sort of—a few images and feelings came back.'

I used to have the dream often, in the years when I first got sick. It was a placeless image. At least eight years had passed, probably, since I had run. Since my body could. And yet this was what I did. Then I woke up. The dream wasn't something you could tell people; it was too much of a cliché. The girl who can't run assumes oneiric capacity and runs— an impossible, desired feat achieved in the way only possible in dreams.

When I had the dream on a regular basis I was still living with my parents, in the cold mountain town, the town full of silence at night, and it was all I could do to walk around the corner. If I could make it to the letterbox at the end of a bitumen lane, ten minutes away, it would be a victory, I'd feel relief. If I didn't take any painkillers, it was a test to get back home. You must save some, as the saying goes. I wasn't good at saving any. Sometimes, on the way back, I would stop, pretend I was looking at something or scratching my foot. I couldn't bend sufficiently to tie my own shoelaces but I could pretend that this was what I was doing. To excuse the stopping, to explain the stopping, because we look at the body and expect it to do things, we expect it to have an excuse when it cannot *do*, as if you cannot just stand still on a street and stare at nothing. There must be an explanation if you cannot return home, if you don't progress in a timely, linear fashion down a country town lane.

There was a house, too, that I'd stop near. It was close to the letterbox. The absolute order of the front garden, the trimmed, evergreen lawn fed by recycled water, the tan-coloured bricks, the gentle spill of a pink-flowered grevillea, was an oasis in the dead-grassed summers of that town. The house wasn't special, not grand or large or new or old, but the green and neatness stilled me. I have always craved a house that is full up with order, stringent in its calm suggestion of nothing too great or overdone. The dream of running was entwined with this house and the walking and the letterbox.

'I'm not sure,' I said, 'if having the dream or parts of it again last night is a sign that I should be moving more, that perhaps I really could run if I tried. Or at least swim.'

Sylvia said I didn't need to be so preoccupied with meaning. 'You had a dream, and you ran. That's it.'

I laughed. 'I don't know why I talk to you like this. It's like I'm talking to myself.'

She laughed too. 'Perhaps it wasn't even you in the dream.'

We finished our coffee, and Sylvia got ready to leave. I didn't know where Sylvia lived or anything much about her life. I knew that, like me, like Frida, she worked at a university—another of so many doublings. She had alluded to some time off: years ago but also more recently.

My university-funded sick leave would end soon, and after a few more weeks of unpaid leave I would return to writing my thesis and short stories, to another round of students, to the office job and the pot plants and fluorescence.

I told Sylvia how, since the hospital, I wasn't sure who I was in those places. I didn't know how to take my body back there. In truth, I'd half-hoped that something would change in my absence and I wouldn't have to return. I don't know what I hoped would happen—some better job opportunity, or success for my book which meant I wouldn't need to work in an office or teach so much. And yet of course I was going back. Events that raise a person out of their current circumstances are as rare as they are brilliant, and I knew this was an unlikely contingency for me. And so reality would require me to find a form for the way I was now—ill but slightly better, recovered but still sick—in the places where I'd worked and studied and taught, even if that form was created from uncertain states and the troubling presence of a mostly invisible illness, and my attempts to control it into absence.

'I know,' said Sylvia. 'I know this too. The truth is we never quite fully return there—but this is a good thing. Trust me, it is. You stay partly with the bit of yourself that left all that behind: work and expectations and . . . I don't know—all the things we call society and *the world*. You realise much of it is necessary in a practical sense, but not essential to who you are. Some of it doesn't matter at all.'

I suspected that Sylvia was in an indeterminate moment, like me; a state of recovery or illness or some other reason that meant she was not active in the way the world expected of her—by which I mean the social world and the expectations on a body of work and movement, assumptions instigated in times when to be in an ill body was to be excluded, shunned from the working roles of others. Now the parameters were vaguer, yet just as threatening: to feel not entirely active in that world and not completely excused from it, as we might be when the illness or injury is acute.

And this is probably how it is: when the condition you have is more a condition you are in, it becomes the condition that you are. In other words, with a case of chronic illness you are in and then out of, communing with and then shunning the world or the social contract, the economic milieu, the structural apparatus. The condition is not a possession given, chosen or had, but a state of being. I could not take it out of me. The disease was a trait of mine, of me, and with it came the hatred and like, affection and indifference we have for the traits that make up our various forms of character.

The time I spent with Sylvia was pleasant yet somehow lined with darkness; sweet and almost guilty. It felt good, the sense of languishing, until I thought about it too much. Even after she'd left the house, I fell into her soft, stagnant way of being. In the mornings, when the old brick house was cold, I sat in the living room with the heater on until my eyelids drooped. Days passed and I wouldn't leave the house, wouldn't even put on shoes. I rarely let myself lie in bed but I wished that I could. Somewhere in me was a profound fear that if I lay down, I would fall too deeply into that idle state. If Tomasz called from work to say he was going to the bar around the corner from his office, I felt deserted, angry, insubstantial. More often than not I'd been inside all day, and I didn't tell him that I did not want either of us to be out there, doing anything. I wanted him to stay indoors too. I wanted him to want nothing more as well. It sounded ridiculous, though I felt just that way.

He would say gently, earnestly, *You should try—come out.*
No, I'd reply. I was annoyed, exhausted with myself or with him, depending on how I felt about the state of rest, and consequently how I felt about Sylvia.

The question of whether to go out in the world or withdraw from it became a point of tension in the weeks that followed. Late one afternoon, Tomasz called me from work. There was an event opening, at a small artist-run space in Collingwood. Would I come? I knew he was eager, impatient.

'I'm okay here,' I said, sure of neither what this meant or whether I wanted to go.

'Why don't you come? I'll get us an Uber home. It'll be easy.'

'I've forgotten how to do things.' I heard a self-mocking laugh leave my throat. 'And I shouldn't spend too much. I'm not getting paid for almost a month.'

'I'll pay, I'll get us an Uber home, promise, it'll be easy.'

'Can't we just have a night in?' I said, aware of how it sounded like a punchline or provocation.

'Please?'

'I'm okay here, honestly. You go.'

'But you don't want me to go.'

'I never said that.'

'You don't *see* people,' he said. 'It's not healthy.'

'I see Sylvia. I saw her today.'

'Our friends.'

'But she is my friend.'

'Fine. I'll see you later. I won't stay long.'

As he hung up, a millisecond too soon, what I felt above all was relief. Tomasz didn't suggest I come out with him for some time after that.

I had tried to tell Tomasz about Sylvia, about the similarities I noticed, the soul-level alignment, the way we were almost beyond words, the two of us. The way we spoke as though we were thinking things out inside our heads. The way our stillness felt complicit and miraculous. How I said things knowing she knew them, the different kinds of saying this entailed.

Tomasz would go out, return home late, get up early again for work. He was so energetic, I was tired of it. It was as though he didn't need to stop, he barely needed to eat. He could disregard his body. Some days I liked to think that this personality was me, too, the one with energy, who got things done. I liked to think this was the person I was. And yet I fought to stay in a state that was for Tomasz a natural one. I did not know what had changed, but recently it was harder to move all over again. I was dragging it, the body. Through the room, through gravity. The days at the pool with Frida were long gone. I stood in the bedroom and stared at its parts: bed and wardrobe and desk, the doors to the balcony. I stared down at my body, aware of myself and my limbs and saliva and stomach. There was wood and paint and me and bone. Tomasz had left for work, he moved and moved. I would wait for him to come home, to come inside, and I wanted him to sit with me. I wanted us to do nothing. It was bad and I didn't know why. Another narrative we have taught ourselves and learned so well: move and do and you will be good.

One weekend we were invited by his friends to the beach, on the south side of the city, close to St Kilda. It was warm, as though autumn had been only a false start, and people kept saying it was too warm; too warm for April. The beaches in the evenings and weekends were different from how they were during the week, in the quiet times when I had been there with Frida. On Saturdays and Sundays the area was crowded, buzzing: music festivals, food trucks, young people playing volleyball. This was what his friends had invited us for—drinks and volleyball, I didn't know in what order. *Come*, said Tomasz. *We can leave whenever you need to.* I was drawn to the thought of seeing the water, even though I couldn't drink beer, it made me sick, and I hated the idea of a ball flying around on the sand, wild and unpredictable. I hated the thought that I was just another person who had aged and grown less confident, athletic, physically active. I saw this change in people and must have subtly judged it, as though some decision was made in the face of the vagaries of time and work, income, capacity in all its many forms, child-raising and stress and ill-health, to let these things win. In my mind these were all impediments or influences that could and should have been managed in order to maintain a primacy of physical condition, to stay fit, stay healthy, stay in control of these things for goodness' sake, as though it were so easy. All of these thoughts and then I said yes to Tomasz, I would go, though it was perhaps only to be near Frida or where I hoped she might be.

The sea, bright and blue when we arrived, was orange-tinged as the sun began to set, and Tomasz's friends arrived for the volleyball game, the drinks. We'd spent the afternoon there together, just Tomasz and I, first at a cafe and then walking along Acland Street, always busy and somehow grotesque in its overactivity—as though the suburb was putting on a show of how Melbourne should appear to tourists: the palm trees and beach view, the grinning face at the entrance to Luna Park, the busy pubs with street-side tables, cafes smothered with graffiti art. I walked close to Tomasz, slightly threatened by the crowds and the low, persistent pain in my leg. After he took my hand, the pain didn't seem so bad.

Tomasz's friends had joined us on the beach. One of the women used a stick to draw a long line in the sand, from where it met the retaining wall and footpath, down towards the water where it became submerged. She moved easily, barefoot, bending down and trotting sideways as she drew. She stood up and laughed. This would be the volleyball net. A few others arrived. Tomasz kicked the ball up and nudged it, knee to knee to foot to knee, agile as always. Tomasz's friend Finn walked over and hugged me. He had a gentle personality, with a suggestion of dissatisfaction or restlessness. He'd had knee surgery recently, and had trouble with the joints in his hands, and perhaps for this reason we seemed to gravitate towards one another at gatherings. He was unapologetic about the fact that he couldn't, or wouldn't, join in the volleyball game. *Nah, not today. My knee is no good.* I wanted to say this too, *My legs are no good*, but I didn't—it would sound like a complaint, I worried. It would sound like I didn't want to be there. With people less known to us it's difficult to integrate daily sufferings into casual encounters. There is a hesitation to lump it all on another. There is a feeling that we should keep things light. Finn and I walked to the water. Tomasz and the others, two women, another man, and Sara, who did not identify as either, ran and leaped and fell on the sand, pausing every now and then to drink beer, their serious, competitive faces suddenly lighting up with laughter.

We stood with the water to our knees. Finn said he was trying to get back into playing guitar; he'd even bought a good electric one second-hand recently. I told him I had tried to take up swimming lately, sometimes in the Carlton Baths, mostly at the hydrotherapy pool. Some days it was easier to go than others.

'That's really good,' he said. 'That would be so good for you.'

'It is good. Not sure how long I'll keep it up, though.' I had not, of course, been to the pool for some time now.

I thought I saw Frida in the distance, standing on the retaining wall where the sand met the footpath, behind her the long line of palm trees on the main road. In the green spaces between the trees, people sat eating and drinking near food trucks. I thought it might be her. The long hair almost to her elbows. Jeans, a white shirt, sandals, and a casual solidity to her pose. 'Canary Island date palms,' said Finn, watching me and then the palms, their huge stout trunks and thick, green crown-like growth. He grinned, holding up his phone, 'I googled it.' In the foreground the volleyball game had petered out, and they all sat to watch the sun setting over St Kilda. The woman walked away before I could decide if it was Frida, and I went with Finn back to the others, relieved that the game was over, the line drawn in the sand to make an invisible net was kicked and blurred, devoid now of its original meaning.

One morning, amid the lingering image of the woman I thought might have been Frida on the beach, I woke up and wanted to be in the pool. I left the house early and took two trams to get to the hydrotherapy pool in Fitzroy. I called the physiotherapist's office on the way: they had a spare place for the morning session; someone else had cancelled just now. My voice sounded so clear and deep it surprised me. The receptionist acted like there was nothing in it and I guessed they must be accustomed to this, to the patients— who were healing, who were sick or in pain—cancelling, postponing, calling at the last minute. I wondered about the person who cancelled, if it was one of the older Italian ladies or perhaps the young athletic woman with the tattoos, or someone else I hadn't met. Or maybe it was Frida—though I told myself she would be there. I cannot explain the certainties I felt then, about Frida, about Sylvia, but they existed.

I imagined the person curled over in their bed, under the covers, having finally made the call they thought about all night or weekend, the *Can I cancel? What will everyone think of me?* phone call. The one that permits the absence, the guilt and its attendant relief.

The ritual came back to me with ease: the stripping-down, cold skin, bathers, and the cold, stark shower, then the pool. The stepping-through and the lukewarm weightlessness. The body adapting, welcoming it, the simple and singular elation of the body being happy. The physiotherapist gave me my exercises and I focused on them, a good patient again. I was good again. Stand on one leg and bend the knee until the shoulders are under water. Repeat five times. Do the same on the other leg. Pursue symmetry. Three walking laps, up and back and repeat, of the small square pool. More and more repetition. Crucial repetition. We were training our bodies in the most miniscule of tasks, underscoring that those things, the everyday movements, fostering the strength of adductors supporting the knees, the balancing potential of the core, were the vital internal beams, unseen and unthought, supporting a cathedral.

And then I saw Frida. She entered the pool with the two Italian women. The moment completed a mirroring: the two older ladies, the two younger, Frida and I greeting one another while the Italian women shared a look, stepping together into the pool.

When Frida said, *It's good to see you back*, and the Italian ladies nodded and smiled, it was as though I'd been forgiven. The feeling of having wronged them all, especially Frida, eased in me.

The good that I felt after the water was ecstatic. It was so good to feel good. I ignored the suspicion that behind all the calm and good feeling was mere relief, that I'd obeyed the hand that pushed me, that I'd stayed just shy of a precipice that day, the other side of which was a loss of control, of not moving at all, of mouldering, warm and immobile, at home. To swim in those public pools was to seek cleansing, forgiveness, in a warm human sea. I emerged onto the steps outside the pool building and was clean, unsullied, finally new again.

The door opened and Frida came to stand beside me. 'Are you in a hurry?'

We walked across the road from the hospital, down the leafy hill past Parliament Station, and sat on low street-side stools outside a cafe in the city. We both ordered black coffee and cold water.

'I'm so glad you're back,' Frida said. 'I don't feel as motivated to go when you're not here.'

A thrill, that she might need me as I did her. 'I'm glad I'm back, too. It was just hard for a few weeks.'

'It will always be hard. There will always be hard times. We have to resist the urge to stop. It's dangerous, the stopping. A slippery slope.'

I swallowed my coffee and nodded, chastised.

'I've finished the physio classes now,' said Frida. She seemed excited to tell me. 'I've been going to the City Baths or St Kilda every day. It feels like a progression. Like I might be getting better.' She looked down at her hands and then back up to me. 'I thought you'd be there. Today was my last recovery class and I thought I might see you, and I did.'

It is difficult sometimes to perceive what you are for a person, when for you they are so much. I didn't quite understand then that I was anything to Frida, that she might need me at all. Frida wore a t-shirt, though the wind was cold. Her hands were bare and dry, her arms goosebumped. From her arms I looked to my own. My skin felt smooth and dry—the warm hydrotherapy water, the chlorine. I felt the fresh air more keenly, the small draughts of cold where my hair was still wet. Frida took out a narrow tube of moisturiser and we slathered our hands and forearms.

'I'll swim every day,' I promised. I couldn't imagine not feeling like I did then. The energy, a hum in the muscles; we felt it, the lightness. I was so thirsty but didn't feel hungry. We would drink another coffee and water, another coffee and water. Frida and I, we were in something, some moment, and I wondered that nobody was watching us and noticing it too. Some height of happiness. Some bodily aspect attained. I didn't want to think that this might be how some people always felt. Surely they would not appreciate the heights.

We met the next day at the old red-brick City Baths building at the northern end of the city. Frida carried a large canvas tote bag over her shoulder. We changed in the humid rooms. Two white women had a conversation with each other and at the same time with their children, who were in the shower stalls, insisting they did not need help, they could take care of their bodies on their own. *Well hurry up, then. We need to leave.* Two older women changed with similar slow but steady movements, their bodies both thin and toned. Compared to the hydrotherapy pool in Fitzroy, at this city pool there was a longer distance to walk from the changing rooms to the foyer to the water. It felt far longer than I remembered it being just a few weeks ago.

'Ready?' asked Frida, picking up her towel and goggles, closing her locker.

'It just feels like a long way back to the changing rooms.'

'You're already thinking about that, aren't you? Remember, you'll feel so different after the pool. Remember the water.'

'I remember the water.'

'You'll make it back.'

'I'll make it back.'

And so we went into the water. It was nearly midday on a Friday and this seemed to be the time for the slower ones, the ones recovering or older or still learning. I was grateful for this, a more forgiving pace. The City Baths were often visited by students from landlocked cities in India and China, who had been warned about the beaches here, the rip-tides unseeable except to the trained eye, told that they must absolutely learn to swim, just as they had been apprised of the ferocity of the sunlight here, the holes in the ozone layer children are told about in school. At the City Baths there were young migrant couples, too, taking their infants and toddlers into the pool, the younger ones developing an assuredness in the water their parents did not have. I thought of the Fitzroy pool and its misspelled Italian *Aqua Profonda* sign warning migrants in the 1950s of the water's danger—migrants like my grandfather, who was then starting his new life, uprooted from Lombardy to Brunswick, and I considered how a pool's occupants change with the gentrifying shift of inner-city suburbs.

Several people walked or stood in the leisure lane. In another lane, preschool-aged children splashed and floated in a lesson. The fast and medium lanes were empty.

We shared a lane and swam back and forth, pausing every few laps to rest and breathe before beginning again. I used the metal steps and handrails to haul myself out of the water in three steps. A primal dripping, warmth and cold. My head thumped wildly, pulsing. My cheeks felt hot. I pressed three fingers over the scar on my hip. Still intact. I followed Frida through the cold of the foyer, with a small limp that I tried to straighten out, pretend wasn't there, to even it out as I walked. I was with Frida. My body could do better than this. We just needed control. I could control this thing that was manifest in the limping, control it into absence. The air was cold, my skin alive. Frida was right: the walk back was not so terrifying, not so far as I'd thought. We stood in the showers, one cubicle each, side by side. Young girls still called out to their mothers, who replied to them through the doors and constant noise of the running water. Others showered in silence. We dressed under the heater in the main room. Then we were outside and the cold was welcome and new, renewing. I thought I could get addicted to it, the chlorine absolution, the strange regeneration born of swimming in that unnatural water: uncommonly warm and too clean, and yet the body, we, adored it.

It felt good. I was back in sync with Frida, alive again. I went to the City Baths three times in one week. Every time, she was there. Frida and I, together. It was miraculous. I came home and Tomasz would say, *Did you swim today?* and he knew already that I had: I was happy when I swam. He asked but he already knew. He could see it in me. It was in my voice and my eyes, my breathing, the steady reverberance and calm. Alive again, emerged from water.

One day when I went to the City Baths I couldn't see Frida there. I told myself there was nothing unusual about this; we hadn't arranged to meet. Yet it was a little unsettling that she wasn't in the pool or the changing rooms or walking up the steps at the same time as me, as often happened. As though I should have been somewhere else, or I'd just missed an important moment. I stepped into the slow lane. In the next lane I saw the young, tattooed, athletic woman from the hydrotherapy classes in Fitzroy. She nodded in recognition and started swimming, far faster than me.

I swam without Frida. I felt slower and thought perhaps I enjoyed it less without her, or maybe it was just my leg getting tired. I had walked to the pool rather than taken the tram, so I'd probably tired myself unnecessarily. I'd wanted to push myself, set one of those insignificant challenges you undertake without telling anybody, and yet feel good or bad about achieving or failing.

In the changing rooms afterwards, the young, tattooed woman said hello. She asked how my body was feeling. I said it was slow, the recovery.

'I can't exercise like I used to,' she said. She spoke to me through every movement the two of us made: our showering, drying, and dressing, brushing our hair. 'I was an athlete. I *am* an athlete—or a former athlete. I don't really know how to characterise myself now. My brother and I were involved in an accident a couple of years ago. I was out horseriding, my brother leading, on the property of some friends of our parents who had land out near Romsey. It was a winter morning, and the fog was thick. My brother stepped in a rabbit hole and injured his ankle, and the horse spooked. It bolted and took us both with it. My brother, with his broken ankle, was dragged. I was thrown off into the fog and crushed my knee.'

I listened. In a similar way to how it was with Frida, I felt no need to react visibly in the ways people do when we speak about pain. We both knew pain as an intimate presence.

'Before this,' she continued, 'I was no stranger to pain. Every month I bleed so heavily I dread sitting on a bus or at my desk at work. Whenever I walk in public I'm sure someone is right behind me, seeing a red mass spread out through my clothes. I bleed through layers and layers and onto my bedsheets. I vomit from the pain of it. The doctor I used to see, a male doctor, would almost shrug, as if to say:

So what? You're a woman; this is your narrative. He would suggest I take painkillers, go on the pill.'

'It's true,' I said. 'There are apparently acceptable forms of pain.'

'What I was not prepared for, crushing my knee like that, was the deep welcoming of my pain. A stranger, out jogging past the property that morning, helped me limp through the fog to the road, and called their partner, who ran back for my brother. He had to be carried out. And then they drove us, the two of them in the front seat, forty kilometres to the hospital. The emergency department on a cold Saturday morning is a revelation. If we could go there just to see ourselves. One great aftermath, the morning after all the nights we've ever had. There was a young man covered in blood, whose friends or siblings told him to sit, sit down, while he kept jumping up, pacing, sometimes almost crying, other times laughing. *I'm good, I'm good*, he kept repeating, coming down from something. A woman with a slurring voice, talking to us all with an ecstatic or pained smile. An old couple, the woman wincing and holding her stomach. A child wrapped in blankets in a woman's arms. Seven thirty am. Every now and then a name was called by a nurse, who would take the person summoned through the doors. A deliverance for making it through the night. When it was my turn, when I was called, I was not prepared for the acceptance of my pain. The doctor murmured, *Yes, yes, it looks painful.* The nurse said, *You've had a rough start to the weekend, hey?*

And they asked how my pain was, on a scale of one to ten, and when I said six they said, *You're a tough cookie—most people would rate that a nine!* And suddenly I was exalted to the status of recognised pain. They gave me painkillers, and I remember'—she held up one hand as if to linger on the memory—'the moment before the drugs kicked in, and at that pinnacle of pain, this thought breaking through: a kind of victorious thought, to have all these knowledgeable people and caregivers crowded around my body, telling me that it was *in pain*, this elevated feeling, the agreement with my body, as though I had passed some test, both spiritual and moral, a test I didn't even know I was about to take, when I put my foot into the stirrup that morning and the horse began to move.'

We had by now dressed in front of each other, made our way out of the changing rooms. She stopped talking for a moment, opened the entrance door. The tattoos across her forearms appeared bolder in colour now, out of the water. We walked down the steps.

'I work from home a lot now and, as I said, I can't exercise like I used to. So I make sure I keep only healthy food in the fridge. I'm competitive with myself like that. I live in a game with many rules.'

I said I understood this; the self-constructed rules, the control. I asked her if she spoke to her brother often.

'He moved overseas, to Europe, a year or so after the accident, chasing a job opportunity, the benefits of which he has extended to me. I now work for the company, entirely online and sometimes in the middle of the night, so I can align with his time zone. I know he has problems now with his ankle, and he can't play soccer or run like he used to. He has never blamed me and yet . . .

'We mostly talk as colleagues now, rather than as brother and sister. Maybe the worst thing, the thing we never mention in our pain, is that the horse was killed after the accident. It broke its leg. The family friend whose property we were visiting didn't call a vet to euthanise it humanely, or even sedate the animal. It was shot in the midst of its convulsive fear in that fog. I thought of it often afterwards, imagined it so often it's become a memory. The animal's eyes horrified at the sight of our friend walking towards it, the gun and the fog.

'We both have this ongoing pain, shared but completely separate, this thing that joins us like our blood.'

We walked towards the nearest train station. At an intersection, she stopped and studied me closely. Her eyes were green with gold-lit brown flecks. She said, 'I could never work out why you were in the classes. You look so normal. I couldn't figure out what was wrong with you.'

I shrugged and said that was the nature of the disease. It showed itself in some external ways, but mostly on the inside. I asked her whether she and her brother might be simply beyond words, having reached a level of shared experience that did not require restating or analysing after the accident. She shrugged and we kept walking.

'He's never returned home since the accident. I stayed here. It sounds silly, but when it's coming into summer over there, like now, and it's getting cold here in Melbourne, I feel more cut off from him than ever. I want so much to be in the heat. We both hate the cold—even more so since the accident. It's harder to move. I see him, my brother, over there and ecstatic with summer. On weekends he drives to the lakes. The rich deep blue pools in the north of Italy, where teenagers gather on pontoons, smoking and laughing and playing music on their phones; where old Italians swim lengths with their tanned, wrinkled skin, and fishermen pull out coral-pink trout, thrashing as they drown in the air. When he sends photos or video-calls me, I'm sure his pain is less than mine. I should say that I feel relieved for him, and of course a part of me is—the moral voice that knows I should be happy for another—but for the most part I feel split off from an aspect of myself. Detached. Here in the cold. I feel jealous—enraged, even. I have to end the conversations as quickly as possible. I have to walk while I talk to him, so that I can tell myself at least I'm exercising while he's lounging around eating. My competitiveness towards myself is integrated, infused with my competition against him. It feels the same. As though he is me.

'It goes the other way, too. If I have a day when I feel good, and he feels bad on that same day, I don't want to talk to him. I ignore his messages for as long as possible. It's difficult when we must work together and he seems unwell, because I just want to say to him: *Go for a walk, a swim, don't drink so much beer and grappa, eat better. Fix it. Fix yourself.* I put that pressure on him, in my mind; I judge him, because his condition is on par with my condition. If he cannot fix himself, this is an omen of my own future. This sounds awful, but I somehow think you'll understand.' She looked at me, her striking green eyes.

I said I could understand. They were familiar to me, the feelings she described. She didn't mention Frida and I wondered if she knew her. We said goodbye at the station entrance.

'I hope it works out for you,' she said. 'I hope you get better.'

I went back to the pool that Sunday, in the morning. I didn't see Frida. I swam laps and went through the motions, the undressing and showering, the drying and dressing. The emergence out into the air afterwards. It was so good to feel good, I craved the water every day. I told myself I didn't need to see Frida there every time; I would do it alone. Yet it seemed to me I craved the water less when I didn't see her, as when you have a new, bodily-absorbing crush and each event or day without the object of that crush seems pale, prosaic.

I heard Tomasz telling someone on the phone, perhaps a friend or his mother, that I was *doing really well*. Perhaps it was merely recovery. All that miraculous feeling, the obsession with the pool, the elemental connection to Frida. People told me I was recovering. *You won't know yourself,* was what they said. They uttered phrases that sounded commercial, clichéd: *Like new. Good as gold. Well again.* Meaning soon, meaning healing. But this presupposed that I had ever really known myself or that the self I knew best was some version back in time, the version most ill, and to be better would be to form a new self.

This seemed to insinuate, too, that the moment of self-knowledge would soon pass or had already passed; I knew myself best when I was in the greatest pain and every movement was dictated by its presence or potentiality, or when I was in the hospital, sleeping through the day, awake through the nights, the uncertain space between pain and recovery, oscillating between the two, never concretely in either state. This thinking—*You won't know yourself*—suggested that those states of pain or oscillation were me, were the truth.

When I had considered writing about my illness, which I had mostly avoided, I read an interview with the writer J.M. Coetzee. I have forgotten the content save for what he said about Dostoyevsky's ideas on writing the self. Summarising Dostoyevsky's beliefs, Coetzee said: *What is self-delusional is to imagine that you can tell the truth about yourself, that it merely takes a certain frankness with oneself and a certain boldness in putting things down on paper and revealing them to other people.* The confessional, the faithfully factual, would not, it seems, convey the truth—or would be only one ingredient of it.

A recovery robbed of certainties entails a partial venture back to what one knows, the body and brain ever the same and utterly different as the cycle of illness turns, hooks into the skin, snags the self ever back to it. Representing such a state would forever be in its own cycle of identification and de-identification, familiarity and estrangement.

When I seemed better, Tomasz seemed happier. I went out more often with him. There was less of the hesitation or vexation in his voice when he suggested meeting friends or going to a restaurant. And it's true that those things had become easier for me. He was playful again, would stand behind me while I brushed my teeth, hug and squeeze me and slip his hands down into my underwear. I would wriggle and laugh if his fingers were too cold or I would kiss his mouth, smearing toothpaste across his lips. Sex in the shower, on the edge of our bed, none of it seemed too much for my body or too much of a risk. I believed in my body again, believed that it could. Such things did happen, and I felt like I was well again, like new, good as gold.

In illness and recovery, and perhaps any single consciousness, a worldview is constructed from very small realities. My small realities were: the days when I swam and those when I didn't. My self-narratives, making or ruining a day or otherwise tinting it.

One day I walked instead of going to the pool and I saw Sylvia. I can't explain why I walked when I should have swum again, and again, so preserving the appearance of routine, but that day was different, I was different. Was I relieved to see her? She was sitting on the park bench and waved me over. I was relieved to sit down, aware of a frustrating tightness in my neck and shoulders, reaching up over my scalp. The place where we sat really wasn't far from the house, barely a five-minute walk. Even so, we'd both had enough and she walked home with me. I began to think that the two of us only walked in order to see each other, that I only walked so that she could walk me home again.

I made coffee. I'd purchased a box of fruit and vegetables, delivered to the door a day earlier. There were six bright tangelos among the green leaves, the earthy brown vegetables. I took one out for each of us. We sat on the balcony together. My head ached. I was so glad to be sitting, so glad that Sylvia let this happen. The relief of it. Sylvia wore gloves and scratched her hands through the wool, an action both brittle and soft, but she wouldn't say a word about it. We watched the people who could not see us as they walked beneath the balcony. We knew nothing about them.

'If I was to see myself in this way,' said Sylvia, looking down at a woman walking past, 'I wonder how I would appear. Our own body, excised of thoughts, is not something we're used to comprehending.' Sylvia chewed her top lip and gave a small laugh. 'Twenty metres away from myself.' She looked at the ginkgo leaves, their bright yellow. 'I think I'd be fond of her, mostly.'

With her gloved fingers, Sylvia began to remove the orange peel from the tangelo, then the cobweb-like membrane. A single woollen thread attached itself to the tangelo flesh and Sylvia had difficulty picking it off. I looked away. A tangelo can't be eaten neatly, can't be sliced like an orange; the segments have thin skin that breaks at the gentlest touch. Our thumbs pierced the crescent moon pieces, juice leaked liberally over us. I let it bother me, the sticky skin, I hated feeling dirty, and I thought about getting up to wash it off. Sylvia looked down at her own chest, smiled and shrugged at the drops beading on the wool, on her chin. I smiled too, like a schoolgirl with a new friend, wanting to be just like her. In many moments, I wanted to be just like her.

'I have bad nights,' said Sylvia. 'Do you have them too?'

'I have bad nights,' I said. They were elongated, cavernous, and although during their course fears tended to multiply, at times I loved them, those nights.

'I sometimes love them too,' she said.

'I can never tell anyone these things. I love them because I'm alone and close to just myself.'

'And now close to me.' She said it simply, gently.

Pain solidified its presence in the sleeping hours; became a personality that, like some nocturnal vampiric creature, diminished in daylight. It was a familiar personality and it sat closely beside my own—even attached itself. But I would get up, take painkillers, make a cup of tea in the absolutely still and dark house, and I would somehow look back nostalgically on those moments. Maybe it was my capacity to romanticise, or it might have been that once pain passed it was hard to believe my memories. Hard to believe that I did love those moments, despite the pain. They were mine alone.

Sylvia and I only ever sat on the balcony. The sunlight was yellow and bleached up there, giving my memories of Sylvia both a dim and overexposed light. She hadn't met my housemate, or Tomasz, and this seemed to suit our singular, enclosed form of friendship. It suited our perspective of ourselves. In fact, she had never asked much about Tomasz or expressed a desire to meet him. For some reason this relieved me. I liked that Sylvia liked the balcony. Each time she came to visit she said, *Should we go and sit on the balcony?* The ginkgos were still yellow, but starting to fall from the trees.

'Tomasz says we should sleep out here one night,' I said. 'We might have to wait until summer.'

Sylvia talked about Victorian-era houses, how some used to have sleeping porches, because sleeping outside was thought to be good for tuberculosis patients. Later, medicine determined that night air was bad for us, dead organic matter floating around and making us sick. Freud, when he was dying in London, spent a lot of time in his light-filled loggia—a covered space in the large back garden in Hampstead, a place both interior and exterior, where he could be suspended between worlds, sitting outside under shelter.

'I don't know why I went to the park today,' I said. 'But I'm glad I saw you.'

'Maybe you didn't feel as well as you thought you did. Maybe the park was just what you needed.' She pulled her chair closer, rested her head on my shoulder, her woollen sweater soft against my arm. 'We are the same self,' she said, resting her gloved hand on mine.

Autoimmune comes from *autós*, Ancient Greek for *the self*, and *in-munis*, Latin for *no longer in service*. Immunity is to build up a fortification, a defence. This disease therefore represents an attempt to protect the self from the self, the use of body as weapon and shield, and failing. A body not in service to itself. We must watch it move in the mirror of the self. Friend and enemy move together in a biting dance, against each other. There is both proximity and destruction. Nudge the mirror. Embrace as you fall over the cliff. Metaphors proliferate as I write, I can't help myself. I can't help my self. The self as cause and creator. It is all too easy to write in literal metaphors, falsely concrete terms.

I decided that tomorrow I would go to the park again, so that I could see Sylvia again. I wouldn't go to the pool, I wouldn't swim.

I woke early. I sat in bed drinking coffee.

'Did you have a bad night?' Tomasz asked. He breathed heavily, his body and breath warm with sleep.

I shrugged and said it was my leg. I also wondered, faintly guilty, if Sylvia's talking about bad nights had in fact brought this one about.

'You knew. You helped.'

'Really?' He didn't remember, was only vaguely aware of my restlessness.

In the night, as happened sometimes, Tomasz—or rather his body—knew that I was awake and that I didn't want to be, shifting and breathing and sometimes making faint sounds of discomfort, because often feeling needs another form. His hands at these times found me and massaged my neck, my hip, in between my eyes, and though he was asleep he was conscious in other ways—in some bodily way. On any bad night I preferred this, his nocturnal awareness, to him waking entirely, as though it gave me access to some subconscious place we couldn't share in our daily lives.

He always slept well, solid nights through.

'You knew,' I said, and he was as surprised as if I'd said a stranger had come in the night and caressed me, because he didn't remember, meaning the conscious waking mind of Tomasz didn't remember those night encounters when one body called to another, *I am hurting*, and the other body answered, *I am here*.

He was to go on a bike ride with his friends that day, and I was in awe of it, always, the way he could be so confident about what he and his body were going to do. Even if the activity involved discomfort, muscle pain, fatigue, it was something they sought, these riders, because they knew in a visceral way that their bodies could perform the act and would do it and they would come home again and feel yet better afterwards, after showering and eating and relaxing, drinking a beer, groaning deeply. I didn't know that pain, that muscular, groaning fatigue. They'd return like that and I'd stare at them. I'd watch Tomasz.

I didn't know, could not recall, such faith in the body, nor how it felt to submit to a testing kind of pain that would make one stronger. A sense of absoluteness towards the body. Progression rather than degeneration. I was not envious, I told myself, because such feats were simply not attainable for me—as though envy required an ingredient of possibility.

He was gentle, with kisses, and then was up and out of bed, getting dressed, shorts and jersey and socks.

'Are you swimming today?' A sip to finish his coffee.

'I'm going to the park. I'll see Sylvia.' My voice sounded slow. My head felt thick with fatigue.

'Which one is that, which friend?'

'My park friend,' I said. 'Sylvia is my park friend. Frida is my pool friend.'

'All these new friends,' he said, kissed me on the forehead, tucked his keys into the back pocket of his jersey. 'Will I ever meet them?'

'One day, maybe.'

'Just rest,' he said.

I watched his lithe body, known and unknown to me. The loss that came with his leaving, so sudden and early in the morning, shook my body. A flash of jealousy after all, perhaps. In comparison to him I was a statue, I was lazy. I wanted to align my body with his like I used to, align myself with him. And then he was out the door. I drank my coffee. The jealous bodily instant passed.

It was one of those days, I realised, that required a lot of calculation. I was heavy and grey. My body. My leg. A little coffee left, dregs in the bottom of the cup, enough to swallow the paracetamol crushed with my back teeth. I kept the tablets on the small shelf beside the bed and I kept them orderly, always sealing the small waxy cardboard box, the familiar image of pill packets open and discarded and piling on bedsides, accompanying stagnant glasses of water, tissues, food wrappers, was to me intolerable evidence, some fearful stereotype, of all control being lost.

Did I cause this bad day, with my decision the night before not to swim? Or did my body know its state, this increasing pain, before *I*—or whoever is this conscious mind—knew too? These were the things I obsessed over.

I waited for the lifting, the slight relief, to come from the pills and then calculated the steps, the places, the action, the steps. The calculation. The holding on to things. The things to hold on to, to help the steps. One step to the wardrobe, two more then hand to the mantelpiece, and then the two more steps to the door, as though grasping for balance on a ship at sea, hand to the doorhandle and then to the wall, wall, wall to bathroom, and then I stood under the water, falling heavy and warm. And then I made my way back with one hand to the wall, wall, wall, into the bedroom.

Hand to mantelpiece. Tomasz out riding, ascending, moving. Dressing was slow; I regretted the shower. Hand to bed, sitting on the edge. Tomasz riding, sweating, wheels spinning. Some days I didn't bother showering, I could not bear the slowness; the perception born of anger, of fatigue and internalised biases, that it was an indignity to struggle with the act of undressing, the showering, the necessity of dressing. I remembered my mother putting on my socks for me just months ago, just thirty years ago, me being confused about wanting the care, the consolation that came from someone doing this mere yet significant task for me while being embarrassed by it, struck down by it, sad for my mother over it.

    I put on my socks. I'd evolved a technique of using just one hand to hook the material on my toes, left hand to left foot, elongating the torso on the right side, compressing the ribs on the left in order to put on the left sock, then repeating for the other side. Easier for the bra and jumper. The loose jeans took some time. And I was, finally, dressed. Did I really need to go out? The leg. The bad night spent. But I did, and I did. I went.

Sylvia was there at the park, just as I'd hoped. Of course she was. I sat beside her on the park bench, the Children's hospital behind us, the playground and trees in front. Beyond that, the city existed in rectangular peaks and morning reflections. Her eyes looked tired and shadowy, her hair, tied back in a loose bun, was limp and dirty. When she hooked her elbow through mine, her arm felt heavy.

'You didn't have to walk today, you know,' she said. 'Your leg.'

'It's good for me to walk.' I must have sounded defensive.

'But all the thinking before the walking, the thinking about the walking. It's so much. The walking, the anxiousness, the leg. Maybe it's not worth it. Maybe you did something you didn't really want or need to do.'

She said things I thought or did, but did not say or admit to myself. Sylvia expressed them in new ways; I hadn't seen them from that perspective. The view ahead was the trees, the playground, the city beyond. It was still early enough to be morning, still dew and coldness in the hours I loved, when the day still felt possible, before too much time had passed and I found myself exhausted all over again.

'This view,' I said. 'I like it. The morning.'

'Nothing has happened yet. Things might still happen.'

I told her about all the calculating: the walking, the hand on the wall to wall, wall to door, hand after hand. When I was in all those thoughts there weren't many ways out.

'And yet you came here.'

'It's hardly a walk.'

'You found a way out.'

'I need to go out. Don't you feel the need to go out?'

'Not really,' she said. 'But then here I am, every day, waiting for you.' Sylvia's voice, deep and sweet. Sometimes sharper, just a little, when she knew what she wanted. Like when she said, 'Let's go home. To the balcony. I love the balcony, the sun, the sitting inside, the sitting outside.'

Her voice I felt as a dark amber colour, shot through with sunlight.

'I'm telling you, let's go.' Was she annoyed? In pain herself? When she stood, our arms still hooked together, I stood too.

As we walked my leg stiffened. I walked slower, Sylvia walked slower; the painkillers wearing off. She spoke gently. She suggested again that perhaps it wasn't such a good idea, the walking, the steps, going out to the park. I didn't want to snap at her but I could have, I wanted to, the frustration of it, and maybe I knew she was right and maybe she knew I wanted to snap at her because I was already doing it with my mind-muttering thoughts, cracking inflamed thoughts that were often ugly and sometimes shocked me with the bitterness rearing in them. Was I really that angry? Those apparently commonplace acts—the walking, the going outside, the small exertions—had a heightened significance. Redolent of a moral compulsion and compliance, a duty and its satisfaction or failure. I couldn't abide the failure. I could not stand it.

'Why do you go out then, Sylvia? Why are you here?' I thought I did sound angry.

'Stop doubting me,' she said, her voice perhaps a little sad. 'You know I only want what's best.'

'I'm sorry—I'm sore.'

She smiled. 'So am I. I'm angry too. Sometimes. All of the time. Because we didn't ask for this.'

'We didn't ask for this.'

'It's acceptable to be angry.'

'We didn't ask for this and it's acceptable to be angry.'

When illness is invisible, the pain manifests in behaviour, behaviour speaks you. Unwitnessed wound, behaviour is the way you say it all. The brain learns pain—I have read this—which makes chronic cases particularly hard to fix. The problem is no longer just isolated body parts, inflamed joints of a haywire immune system. The person is the pain with the whole of their brain and central nervous system. It is learned behaviour. Entwined with personality in this way. The person becomes quick to anger, quick to fear, quick to judge, cannot receive criticism, cannot cope with change, cannot control disproportionate emotional responses. The person—and here I may be talking about myself, about Sylvia, about Frida—develops a worldview structured by pain. Pain dictates perception dictates capacity. Meet the task or shield your face with your hand. I had to meet it. I didn't have to meet it. This doubleness was me.

When pain is chronic, subsumed into daily experience, it becomes another thing you do: breathe and feel hungry; hurt and wake up and go to sleep; hurt and have sex and orgasm; ache and go to work and make small talk; laugh and have conversations with others; be drunk or be sober;

hurt and love and ache. It is being. It is being and so it must have language. A trait of character. It is different, is what I mean. The chronic state is different, a distant cousin to fleeting pain.

Sylvia walked me home. Sylvia walked me through these thoughts and didn't disagree with me. She didn't come inside that day, because it was the weekend and the others would be home, or for some other reason. She said goodbye and suggested I try not to have such a distrust of rest. And I felt so tired, the walking, so bitter, the leg, the hip, the neck, that I wanted to believe what she said. Overwhelmed, I closed the door, walked down the hallway; the wall, my hand, the wall, into the small kitchen.

Tomasz returned from his bike ride, energised and clear-eyed. The day got colder. By afternoon the blue hour rain was absolute, ending the day early. Tomasz worked in his cramped workshop. From the kitchen, I could see his yellow light through the rain. I sat inside and stared at my fingers as they ached dully, and I thought of Sylvia, mostly with warmth. I was aware then of conflicted feelings—most troubling, the sense that I could not get away from her.

I spent a week of nights awake. I spent a week of nights. Alone and his sleeping figure comforted me. Tomasz next to me, sleeping. His breathing and the instances his body knew and found mine, a hand reaching, to comfort, an act he never remembered. Even from my perspective inside the pain, it was easy for me to adore the mercy and beauty of those small lonely moments that the night, in forming itself, slowly bled out.

I tried to write about this at the time. Every attempt was impossible—boring, it seemed to me. There was no real narrative, no peak or depth in the sameness of each day in pain. A cyclical disease does not allow sufficient linearity or propulsion. I wanted, in other words, to make something as inconstant as my self and body.

One day I couldn't get my ring on, the one with the citrine stone. The middle finger of my right hand. I thought of the Irish doctor who first treated me. Her hands were a metaphor of old trees. Knuckles bulged and frozen, fingers stuck in dancing poses. Renoir's hands. *The drugs didn't exist when I was a girl,* she'd said in her gravelly, melodic Irish accent. The woman was thin in a gamy, unhealthy kind of way and it obsessed me, the abjection apparent in her body and the aversion I felt towards it. I obsessed about her fingers and wrists and hands. Mine looked okay and untroubled then, and this made me obsess more, project to some feared future.

I put the ring on a finger on my left hand instead. There was nothing I could do. I swallowed it down and went down the steep staircase. When I was awful and Tomasz said, *What's with the mood?* I said, *Nothing.* Nothing outside of the body.

We went to bed early that night; I guessed he was disappointed that I couldn't keep my eyes open. His friends had invited us for dinner, but the prospect terrified me and I said I was sore, I didn't want to go. He said he would stay in too, knew something was amiss, and the relief, the relief until next time. I'd realised social encounters were for me mostly about control. When unenjoyable it was because I had lost any handle on my physical situation, whether from pain or the fact of needing to be like everyone else, stay out later, sit in this or that cold and uncomfortable place. The relief of avoiding such things was akin to maintaining control.

Mid-morning one day when Tomasz was at work, I opened the door and there was Sylvia, her blonde-auburn hair tied in a loose side ponytail. She wore black linen pants and a loose, dark blue, half-zip jumper.

'It's my hands,' she said. She held up a brown bottle, some kind of ointment or lotion. 'They gave me this stuff for my hands and feet. I don't know what to do. I can't . . .' She said my name.

'Come in.'

I made coffee and gave Sylvia a tall glass of cold water. A doctor had recommended that she wash her feet and hands with the ointment, to soothe the skin and to stop an infection forming.

'I'll do it,' I said. 'I'll wash them.'

'I don't want to look at my hands and feet,' she said. 'Hideous! I don't want them to be mine.'

'I'll wash them,' I said again. I kept repeating this, feeling like a mother offering a soothing mantra. 'I'll wash them.'

We went up to the balcony. She'd never let me see her hands. I had to, or it seemed that I had to, hold one of her wrists firmly and wrest the woollen sleeves from her clutching fingers. I was reminded of my mother, when I visited her at the nursing home where she worked, and old June, the lady who sat in a far corner seat in the sun, and the way my mother prised open her clawed hands to cut her dug-in nails. Sylvia's hands were white and covered in a dazzling red rash. Her knuckles looked a little red and swollen, but I couldn't tell if this was just the rash, or if the disease had reached the joints in her hands. I told her that it happened to me too, the flaming red, the relentless itching before the drying, the cracking, and the weeping.

'Of course it does,' she said. 'I knew you would know.'

I washed her hands. Dipping and wringing a cloth, patting and rinsing. And then her feet. It was relaxing, the repetitive action, it reminded me of breathing.

I washed her hands once more, and she said she liked the cool feeling, the relief of it.

'I almost didn't come here,' she said. 'I couldn't sleep because of it; I feel like I'm on fire. Like some part of me is. Where does all our heat come from, this burning?'

I shrugged. 'It's inside us. It's nobody's fault.'

'I want to believe you,' she said. In almost a whisper she added, 'Sometimes, I just rest and rest and sleep and I can't remember what it feels like to move. Where do you go, when you don't walk in the park?'

And then I said what I perhaps shouldn't have. I said I had a friend, another friend, named Frida and that sometimes we went swimming. It was the first of several unsettling eclipse moments: I brought one of them into the sky of the other. Should I have left them separate, could I have left them separate?

'You swim with her. The other one. Do you talk about us? You know, it's not particularly healthy to go out as much as you do. Is she forcing you?'

'I need to move, Sylvia. It's good for me. I love the pool, I get obsessed with it sometimes.' I realised I had no way of telling Sylvia what it meant to me, the pool and its absolution, the sense of control and goodness.

'This doesn't really sound like you. Don't forget your pain.'

'Why not?'

'Pain is not *you*. Or me. It's something we have. And sometimes it must still us. We are still us.' She grinned. She loved her poetic turns, her word play.

We held each other's hands. I realised I had the beginnings of the same bubbling red sores on the palms of my hands, on my ankle and heel, a telling marker of the disease we shared. The gradually persistent, warm itch. I hadn't noticed it starting.

'I'll wash them,' said Sylvia, taking up a fresh cloth and bathing my palms.

I know that Sylvia washed my palms and feet, and there was something tender and ritualistic about it. That I washed her palms once more and she thanked me for helping her. I know that she left the house and Tomasz came home from work. In the night, Tomasz sleeping deeply next to me, a burning and itching took over my foot, a small sore at the ankle turned frenzied. Such a desperate scratching and a strange sleeping pleasure at the feeling of my nails pawing it over and over.

In the morning it was worse. The area around the sore had swelled, the mark itself turned dark red, weeping white and clear. A terrible pain to stand on the foot. My forehead burned.

'What's wrong?' said Tomasz.
'It's my foot.' I raised my leg.
'Shit, that doesn't look good.'
'Should I go to the doctor?'

He put a palm to my forehead. 'You're really warm.' He touched my hand and I knew it was clammy. As had happened before, I couldn't avoid the suspicion that Sylvia had caused this.

The doctor told me to keep washing the wound, took a sample of the weeping pus and told me to rest. I lay in bed for two days and felt delirious, too hot, scratching and sore. The whole foot swelled and I could barely look at it, this foreign thing, not me, myself estranged. Tomasz called the doctor, who said to go to the hospital, it sounded bad now.

We sat in the waiting room at the Royal Melbourne Hospital. So close to the parks, the pathways I'd walked with Sylvia. I felt thirsty and dizzy. An elderly couple sat opposite us. The man was pale, his eyes red, while the woman watched him and seemed never to blink. Next to them was a young pregnant woman, holding a toddler. They called me through after three hours. The doctor asked if it was possible the wound was a spider bite, had I noticed any spiders in the room, in our linen or clothing, could I have been bitten in my sleep? I said I had no idea, I didn't think so.

Something had caused this fevered immune response, and they didn't know what it was.

'Your body is going into overdrive,' said the doctor. She told me about the various tests they would perform, all of which I forgot straightaway as I lay there, feeling little more than a hazy mind observing this body from afar. My foot as pink as raw meat. The sore was covered but leaked such amounts of pus and fluid a nurse had to change the dressing every few hours. When I told someone the medication I was on, they seemed to think this was significant, and called for a specialist who took hours to arrive. He confirmed that yes, it was probable the medication was behind it all. Compromised immunity, lowered capacity to fight infection. Which meant in effect that it was my body itself causing all this trouble, not some external threat of nature like a spider. *You were told about these risks, right?* said the specialist flatly.

We'll have to keep you overnight, someone else said, and I was conscious of Tomasz kissing my forehead, telling me he would bring coffee in the morning.

And then the long night alone, unsleeping, a cannula line sending hydration and antibiotics through my arm, which turned numb with the cold liquids that took hours to seep into me from the bags hung on a hook and pole. The hospital again. Eternal fluorescence, the night noises, humming and beeping and footsteps and voices.

The hospital again. The harsh lighting of the emergency department, the lack of windows, gave me the feeling of being underground. Lying there, hours and hours, in a tiny room alone, watching the bags of liquid and the clear line, the hallway almost silent now, three o'clock in the morning and everyone mostly asleep. Waking from an uncertain doze, I saw a figure at the door, a woman. She paused and looked in, and then turned and kept walking, long blonde-auburn hair nearly to her elbows, a slow shuffling movement as she walked. *Sylvia?* I called. I got up clumsily, movements hampered by the lines of liquid. Pulling the trolley with me, I limped over to the door. My head clouded over, dizzy and swimming. I caught only a glimpse of the woman, the long, wavy hair and the hands hidden in gloves, as she turned the corner and was gone.

Tomasz picked me up the next morning and took me home. I sat on the balcony in the early sunlight. The day was far warmer than the previous one, and I felt slightly better, which felt immensely better. The high dose of antibiotics had stopped the nagging itch and burning in my foot and the swelling had gone down. The sun bathed us, and we could lean back and fall into the dappled shade. I felt truly happy to have that moment.

I told Tomasz how Sylvia sat with me in the same place. How we sat up there with the trees, Sylvia and I. Sometimes a bird would sit on the railing, an orange-beaked blackbird or a myna. It would stare at us, then fly off.

I sat quietly with Tomasz. He looked at his phone and then out at the trees. The scuff of footsteps, the occasional bike wheels on the footpath below. Activewear couples with takeaway coffee cups. Three-year-olds dragging scooters in a feat that looked far more difficult than walking. And then a woman with blonde-auburn hair, long and a little dishevelled, wavy hair that may have been bothered by bedsheets or wind. We saw her and she could not see us.

'Kind of looks like you from the back,' said Tomasz.

'She looks like Sylvia,' I said, my eyes following her. 'Sylvia,' I said just a little louder, but then I was embarrassed. Who knew who that woman was? It could have been anyone, the hair and the jacket. She walked alone and a little slower than someone her age might be expected to walk. I didn't know why this was—who said someone had to walk at a certain speed due to their age, their physical appearance?—but this was my reason for supposing it was Sylvia. *She was shaped just the way I was*, those lines from Plath rang in my head often. The woman walked a little off-pace, you could say, with a slight lilting gait. And then she was gone and Tomasz was ready to move; he never wanted to sit for long.

'Let's go out somewhere, if you feel okay.' And so we walked from Parkville through the university grounds, through the cloistered passageways, along the internal road and over Swanston Street. We sat at a bar on Lygon Street, the plane trees sending small particles into the air, giving the sun-soaked street a glowing, scintillating light. Tomasz drank wine, I had water. We often went to the same places. I adored the regularity that seemed to suit Tomasz in the years we grew our lives around each other. I was addicted to his constancy.

'Is this all right?' he asked. 'Going out like this?'

I put my hand against his face, his cheek and temple and ear. 'It's perfect.'

From the balcony, the next day, church bells. I liked the one o'clock chime best. You couldn't be sure if you'd really heard it or had imagined it, or if you'd heard the remains of the twelve before it, echoing in memory.

Sometimes it happens simply: you wake with energy you have trouble believing and believing in. A week later and I was once again completely in my body, I was in my body in a different way. I felt it. I saw the world with clarity. I knew what I would write that day. I knew where I would go and what I would eat. I saw it all and clearly. Over trivialities I was ecstatic: I drank two coffees, I trimmed my nails short and painted them; the control was beautiful to me, the spectacular calm of ten coral ovals, one at the end of each finger and thumb. Tomasz left for work, our housemate for class. The house was quiet and expectant. I made the bed. I was thirsty, always thirsty; I made tea, hot water with ginger, broth with salt. I could never quench the thirst. Moving from one end of the room to the other was an unthought, expedient thing. It is important for me to remember what I did not think about, or need to think about, on such miraculous mornings—those things essential in absence.

The energy and clarity stayed with me into the week. I spent ever more time at the pool. I continued with the hydrotherapy at the pool near St Vincent's Hospital. I saw different people in the water: a couple of older white men who avoided eye contact and seemed ill-tempered and impatient, whether with their bodies and their vulnerability or the physiotherapist or everyone around them wasn't clear; a Vietnamese woman in her fifties, who was chatty and smiling and whom everyone seemed to adore; a man from Lebanon, I'd heard him say, who bore fresh scars on both knees and joked that his legs were brand-new again, *just like changing a car part*. There was nobody my age this time, and I didn't see Frida.

After finishing the prescribed ten hydrotherapy sessions, it was then the responsibility of the patient to continue to go to the pool, to cultivate the habit or discipline or to give it up entirely. The physiotherapist said it was good, my finishing the prescribed classes, and I wondered if the others I'd met in my first classes—the older Italian ladies, the tattooed woman—had finished them too, like Frida had, or if I'd gone there on different days and missed them by just minutes. Although I hadn't seen her in weeks, I felt close to Frida. I was close to the person I felt myself to be when I was with her.

I went to the City Baths. The cold of undressing, the cold shower rinse, the stepping, dripping, into the pool, ducking down into the lane. I kicked and shivered.

While I rested at the end of the lane, I saw Frida walking through the foyer and into the pool area. She didn't see me. She put her grey towel on a chair, close to where a man watched his partner and child in the water. His clothed, dry body against their close and wet skin created what seemed to me a striking distance between them. Frida went to the pool edge, pausing to breathe and pull her arms back behind her body, stretching out the front of the shoulders, the upper arms. Finally she saw me, walked to the steps and lowered her body into the water.

'Where have you been? I haven't seen you.'

'I haven't seen you,' I echoed. 'Where have you been?'

'In the salt water,' she said. 'The Sea Baths. You should come. You haven't visited me.' Maybe her tone was accusatory, maybe it was a statement of fact.

'You weren't here,' I said. 'I came to the pool, and you were never here. And so I stopped going.' Perhaps my tone was also accusatory, perhaps I was grasping for cause and effect.

'You have to keep going,' she said. And then she nodded towards the lane ahead, dived under the water and started swimming.

There is a loosening, a reacquaintance and return, when a body meets water again, and it was the same when I was once again with Frida. The body becomes known to you all over again, just as you will always remember water when you return to it. Frida was faster than me, swimming lap after lap, but I was pleased to find I didn't tire so easily; some residual strength remained from those first weeks of swimming with her. Again I felt absolved, the guilt shaken off, and resolved, too, to keep this eternal return in place in my life. It was like this, it still is like this; always such a resoluteness with water, in the water. I will love this always. I will swim always. I said things like this to myself.

And then we were out of the water, Frida and I, chests rising and breathing and falling, the good of it. The sense that I was good for having done good by my body. The return to the body. I'd developed sentiments about goodness and control, and mostly these were about discipline. My neck moved a little better. My knees did too. Some movements had little to no thought behind them, no calculation or anger. The day outside, when I stepped through the doors of the City Baths, standing atop the steps of the red-brick building, was somehow renewed, and with it I seemed less unwell. This is repetitive, but it was and is true—the body and these feelings are just that repetitive. We become bored with it, the body and its demands, frustrated by what it needs again when all it needs is the same good again and again, and more.

From that day on, I saw Frida often. We were at the City Baths nearly every day. She asked if I thought I was getting better. We floated, weightless, at the end of the lane.

'People say I am,' I said. 'They look at me and say that I seem better. I'm confirming the narrative for them. The arc of illness: you're unwell, you go to the hospital, you have treatment, you get better.'

She smiled. 'Tick, tick, tick, you did it all.'

A young man, maybe a student, splashed his way down the next lane in messy strokes. I saw him at least once a week and he seemed to be trying to teach himself to swim, doggedly clawing at the water in strokes too fast to enable him to glide through it with ease.

'The difficulty,' Frida said, 'is that when we want to describe our lives, we look for story, and we're told that stories require beginnings and endings. A start, a plot arc, crisis, and resolution before the end. Illness, when it is chronic, severs these usual links to narrative—we don't have an end point, but we also don't have a moment of transformation.' She lay on her back, looked up at the ceiling, the pool flags, the wooden beams. 'There isn't the beauty of a coda, no orange-gold view like those brilliant skies after a downpour of rain, a sunset that is a recovery, the moment we isolate, that we narrate towards or from. The moment after the crisis when we say, *I am through this, and I am changed. I was sick and now I am better. And here are all the good lessons I learned.* So many narratives tell us this, and we can't relate to it. That's not the story of what is happening to this body here. It is not adequate for the task. There is beginning after beginning and there is no resolution, no end or aftermath. I must swim and swim and swim and each time it is all over again.'

Sometimes a woman came to the City Baths to wash in the changing rooms. The attendants at the desk let her in without paying, a small mercy. The woman stopped me one day as I stepped out of the shower. I was naked, wrapped in a towel. My hair dripped warm. Frida was still showering.

'You look nice and healthy; good on you, love. Take care of yourself, love.' She had an unsteady grasp on words. She said something about her father, an illness, her own body and illness, always being sick. She kept gesturing to her body, now dressed: a zipped tracksuit jacket covering her thin arms, jeans over her hanging fleshy waist and thin legs.

Her teeth were thick with plaque and yellow, her nails long and dirty. I felt embarrassed by my cleanliness, by my organic cotton underwear that I pulled on as she spoke to me, by my sports bathers and my swimming cap, now damp and limp on the seat. She looked at the other bodies in the changing room, muttered to herself, rummaged in the plastic bag she'd brought with her.

After swimming, Frida and I often walked to the State Library cafe. One day, or many, stand out to me. We sat outside. The stone walls were bathed in sun, and university students stood waiting at the coffee cart outside. As the waiter took our order, a breeze lifted his dark hair. When he had left, Frida asked me, 'Where do you go when you don't come here?' Her hair was still wet. The rim from her goggles had traced lines like fatigue circles underneath her eyes. I guessed that my hair and skin looked the same. 'You were fine, that last day I saw you. And then you didn't come.'

It is hard to describe the odd mix of guilt and motivation Frida inspired in me. I didn't want to offer her weak excuses. I really didn't. There was a sense that she was right, that she would always be right, in a way somehow moral and bodily.

I told her about the day when I went to the pool and swam alone, without her, how I felt very different, heavy and cumbersome in the body. And how, on the days I didn't go to the pool, I rested, or tried to rest, or I walked. I said that often I didn't feel like I possessed the same body from one day to the next. And again I said what I perhaps should not have. I said I had a friend, another friend, named Sylvia, and that sometimes she visited. Again I brought one of them into the sky of the other. Should I have left them separate, could I have done so?

'What do you do with this other friend?' Frida asked me.

Later, I repeated her line to myself and always it was said curtly, even suspiciously, but I didn't know if I could trust my reconstruction.

'We sit on the balcony at my place. We drink coffee, talk.'

'Is that all?'

'We don't really do anything. We meet in the park sometimes.' I felt ridiculous, laughable, like I was a girl again and scared of making my friend jealous. Worse was that I realised I had no way of telling Frida what it meant to me: the balcony and the moments of nothing, of rest. The unbinding of discipline. The shirking, finally, of compulsion. Meaning Sylvia and everything she was to me.

'This doesn't sound like you,' Frida said, shaking her head. 'It's not healthy to sit so much with her, to talk and think so much.' It was the first time she had seemed possessive.

'I can't be like you all the time, Frida.'

'It's a choice. I choose to be like me.'

Later, I would be sure that her voice was curt this time. It's a *choice*. The monosyllabic resonance. It's a choice. She might have seen that I was upset or otherwise sick of the conversation; in any case, she stopped talking. It's a *choice*, she had said, and I was not sure if I believed her.

How can a body be so different from itself? That very day, so unlike the body I had with Sylvia, the one in which I was close to my interior self, my self languishing, resting, body cloaked, woollen jumpers warm on warm skin, long moments of stasis. The hot sun on the balcony. From that vantage I looked at her, at the woman I was with Sylvia, and I looked back, at the image of me there with Frida, swimming, and she, both women, were strangers to me.

Frida and Sylvia. Being with them was being a certain person. It is like this. With others, we become alternative versions of ourselves. We become so many people when we walk out the door, when we face the street and see our friends and talk to strangers and colleagues and speak to our loved ones and then again when we lie down at night. I am all of them. And this has always been the difficulty.

The American photographer Francesca Woodman photographed herself hundreds of times in her brief career, and yet critics debate whether this was strictly, or at all, self-portraiture. The art critic Arthur Danto argued that she presented a range of characters, all named Francesca. He believed that she invented a character, the fictive life a metaphor for Francesca's own inner life. Another critic, Marco Pierini, disagreed; for the woman in the photographs to be a credible character, there would need to be a *detachment between the two Francescas,* and this was not perceived in the work or the process. Rather, the portrait *finds its truth precisely in that subjective inner life of the artist from which the necessity of the work of art originates.*

Frida and Sylvia. We exist in others. We exist in the *Blue Nudes* drawn by Henri Matisse from his wheelchair following surgery for stomach cancer. He drew them first and then cut them from paper because this was a way he could create art while sitting down; it was the art he could create from the body, from inside the body he had. Meaning: this was the art he could create.

I imagine him sitting there, directing his helpers to transfer his drawings onto large sheets of paper and create lithographs from his cut-outs. I see us, Sylvia and me, in the *Seated Blue Nude No. 2.* One leg folded on the ground, the other bent in front of her, the head tucked protectively under the right elbow. I see Frida and me in the *Blue Dancer,* our body bending and apparently weightless; of course we are in water. It is such an effortless distinction, the sitter and the swimmer. It is facile, perhaps, to find ourselves in artworks like these, reproduced in their hundreds of thousands. But we do. I have seen so many new and second-hand versions of these prints for sale online. Each time I see them, I want to buy them, so cheap, simply framed, seemingly accessible and suitable for any interior space. I see them as Frida and Sylvia, but then I think of just how many of them there are in the world and I feel wary of the multiplicity, the potential for inauthenticity, and I am yet to buy them.

Frida waited at the Sea Baths in St Kilda. If we wanted to swim in the ocean, we could pay an extra few dollars for wristbands from the reception desk, permitting us to go in and out of the back door that led from the tiled floor to the sand. To the sea. On some level it was ridiculous, paying to swim in nature. But I loved the idea of it, the to-and-from, warm bathing to wild cold water and back again. It was late autumn, the cold air completely still, a still-warm sun. Rare clouds.

    I started to learn the faces of the people who swam and bathed indoors. And I loved this, as though I too belonged now. Old couples with a touch of glamour met to talk and take in the hot water of the spa. The women were thin or had bulging knees, full lips and European accents, some wore blush and lipstick carefully kept away from the water; the men had pot bellies and concave chests, some with thin gold or silver chains around their necks and wrists. A woman with soft, dyed hair, a dark red-brown, kept her head raised carefully above the water, protecting her loose, styled curls from a single drop of water. They were forty, fifty years older than us, those St Kilda and Balaclava regulars who met and talked and gripped the handrails firmly to get in and out of the water, and probably they arrived in the city, fled here, before or during or after the war, yet I felt that I knew their bodies, or perhaps I mean their way of being in the body, more than the young, fast swimmers in the lap pool, or the ones who donned neoprene socks and caps and braved the outdoor sea.

For a few weeks or more, right into the winter, I visited Frida every day. Mostly we swam in the city or at the St Kilda Sea Baths. On a strangely warm winter day, when it was nearly nineteen degrees, we went first to the open water outside. As we walked across the sand Frida asked about my leg. Was it out of concern for me, or expectation? A question that preoccupied me. I wanted to confirm the story she wished to hear: that I was healing. I did not ever want to disappoint her. *It's okay.* I said that my fingers had been swelling lately, that I'd had some days when it was hard to move, to make myself move, but I saw Frida look towards the water, the lulling and calling sea, and I said quickly that maybe I hadn't been trying hard enough, had drunk more wine and sweet drinks lately, as though blaming the body's capacity or incapacity on my lack of mental will or effort, and despite the danger of such thinking, I sensed this was a truth Frida might believe in. *The water is good for you,* she said, *it's so good for us.* Frida tucked her hair into her swimming cap and shook out her shoulders. We stepped into the cold water. A vastness opened in me. How fake the pool and its chlorinated warmth. This was real. *I could love this,* I told her, but she had swum away, her ears full of salt water.

I'd never been one for oceans. I liked the water well enough, but the depths and their lack of control had always terrified me. The sudden darkness of a cloud passing over. As a child, on holidays, I'd watch other children on the beach at Anglesea. I'd compare, analyse, be in awe of their bodily confidence. Of course I didn't call it that; we don't know the words for these feelings when we're ten, eleven, but it must be significant that we feel them. My act of comparing myself to those other girls' bodies seemed to me to be tied to money. We did not have very much, and alongside my watching of those girls, their lithe and smooth, confident bodies, was an assumption that they had things we did not, cars and holidays far away and nicely carpeted homes, and that they were relaxed about spending money because they didn't need to worry about it (more than any material item or worldly experience, this to me was a signifier of wealth). Underlying this was the incisive schoolgirl logic that the physical confidence, the apparently polished appearance, anything associated with caring for a body, was commensurate with privilege—or that it was one in itself. I would watch them so closely with a sense of fascination, as though my body was watching and learning from another. I had a similar feeling around Frida, of affinity and observation.

Even as the days got colder, Frida often encouraged or pushed me to swim with her outside at St Kilda. She assured me we could come back inside after a short time, into the warm saltwater pools. She was persuasive. The barrier between the warm pool tiles and the cold sand represented a fear embodied and met. We shrieked and laughed at the cold, dipped our heads under the frigid water, the shock of salt on tongue, stinging eyes, and then trotted back up the sand towards the warmth of the baths. We were in our bodies, so entirely. Frida stood at the entrance, feet on the cold sand, facing the sea. She shivered, smiling. That image of her: her shoulders wrapped in a towel, her legs dotted with sand, her hair dripping. The solidity of her figure standing there emphasised who she was, how she was, poised there as if a statue of herself.

When we walked along the beach afterwards I saw people in or near the water. I looked at the bodies along the sand, those walking to the water. I noticed the older ones, the bodies hardy, the mottled skin, an older woman with white-blonde hair in a black bathing suit, with a rounding belly and thin legs, who ran along the sand with a man her age. They had been swimming and now they jogged lightly. I noticed the cyclists in their sixties, the taut sinew of their knees straining and pulling with relative ease as they pedalled along the sea road.

'I think I will swim here all winter,' Frida said. 'I want to push myself beyond what I think is my capacity. If I don't, there's a danger I will stop exercising completely. I would lose my relationship with my body. I would just hate that.'

It was the first hint of vulnerability I'd witnessed in Frida. Of course, I felt the same, lived with the same fear. I told her this. When I was alone, without structure, without movement, I became a person entirely reliant on interiors. I stayed indoors but also became that space in who I was, how I thought and acted. The less I went out in the air, the less I wanted to go out. The less I felt the cold, the less I could cope with the cold. The less I moved, the less I could move.

Frida nodded vigorously. 'The body responds so acutely to behaviour, it's almost as if we're training an animal. The body dictates who we are, how we are. If we train it badly it will be bad. And so I will swim in the winter.' She repeated herself, as she often did. 'I will be cold and my body will learn to be cold. We've come so far in our attempt to obliterate the seasons from our daily lives that this confrontation is shocking, when it should be normal, should be known.'

I was so drawn to her unforgiving seriousness. I would say she believed in things ruthlessly. I felt a new confidence now that the sea was in my head. All the time it was there.

My skin was salty and dry, there was sand in my hair, and I was in this body—this thought returned to me often, *I am here, in it*, that I was in this body, with Frida.

Even if, sometimes, I found the icy cold too relentless, if I happened to feel tired one day, or I felt the heaviness of pain, I pushed myself to keep up with her. I would be back at work soon; I needed to make the most of this time meant for healing. We swam outside, again and again. Just the thought of Frida was persuasive.

We sat on the chairs outside the cafe at the Sea Baths, drank scalding dark coffee laced with ocean, salt on our lips. The breeze found my scalp in cool pockets. Frida's fingers were delicate, sure of themselves, holding her cup of coffee. My hands were less under my control than usual, the knuckles red and sore, and I gripped my cup with both hands. 'You'll get used to the cold,' she said. 'Soon your body will be asking you for it.'

I told her I believed her. I wanted to believe her. My mouth moved slowly, struck by the cold, as though I had to carve the words from marble.

'You'll love this,' she said. 'Trust me, you will.'

It was almost an order, and I nodded, shaking, lips and scalp pinpricked by cold, before she walked me to the St Kilda train station.

'Don't let the cold and the pain make you doubt this. We must always push through it. It's not always supposed to be easy. You'll feel better. It always helps, doesn't it?'

'It does, it does. I'm just cold, Frida.'

'If you let your body control your emotions, you'll feel calm.'

'Don't make me feel bad.'

Frida stepped closer and took me in her arms. It was strange to feel her body against mine; we were not the most affectionate friends. 'I just want what's best for you.' I felt her words murmur through me, her heart beat through me, me and Frida together. Felt my skin and muscles slowly warm, my lips still numb.

Frida said goodbye and I stood in a wedge of sunlight at the station, waiting for the train, and I closed my eyes as though it would help me to absorb the heat, hoping I had not disappointed her.

I did not want to see Sylvia that day. Yet there she was, walking towards me as I came back from the shops in North Melbourne. I had been enjoying the morning. The grey sky suited the suburb: the small Victorian cottages, the brick terraces and warehouses with old faded signs now turned into trendy cafes, the walls coated in electric-pink bougainvillea flowers and Boston ivy. I was full of purpose that morning. I thought that I woke with clarity. I thought that I didn't need the paracetamol crushed with my teeth and that I might even walk all the way to the city, to the Italian cafe I liked. Soon I would return to study and work, my thesis and the short story collection I was supposed to be writing, to the office job one day a week. I was supposed to be returning to the world.

And yet as I walked home, my neck and head felt gradually tighter, and I noticed that, as the minutes passed, the way I felt about that very walk, the beautiful pace and potential of the day, was changing. I no longer had confidence in my ability to enjoy the morning, no longer had faith in the assured potential of the day. In other words, the moment I saw Sylvia was one of the few in my experience that drew such a clear thread between my pain and my worldview, my body and my perspective.

When I said hello to her, I knew my voice was distant, distracted.

'You don't want to see me,' said Sylvia, her soft, glazed voice cracking.

'I don't know who I want to see.'

'You're obsessed,' she said. 'You're obsessed with being one or the other. Why do you want to like her better than me?'

'You're making my neck hurt.'

'You're making your neck hurt.'

I stared at her, silent, stuck where I was.

'Don't split yourself in two,' she said. Her voice was sweet again, dark honey. 'Let's just sit together.'

Sylvia convinced me that my headache was only going to get worse that day. Since the surgery, the leg was slowly getting stronger, but my neck and fingers—it was my neck and fingers now. A point in my neck tightened, and the sensation spread up over my head and pushed, pressed through, I was full of verbs, words, pressing at my eye socket. *I'm looking for the words*, I said. I tried to explain the pain sensation to Sylvia. She agreed that words, descriptions, were impossible, unavoidable.

The balcony, our beloved balcony. We sat there although the sun wasn't out, the clouds a deep grey, stripping everything of colour. Since we had always sat there bathed in sun and warmth, it was now as though I'd taken a wrong turn that day, as if I shouldn't have been there. I couldn't enjoy it out there without the light, without the conditions we were used to, and I wondered how much of reaction is tied to expectation, if the ability to react outside of those preconceptions might be a sign of true freedom. Sylvia's hands stayed hidden in her woollen sleeves, mine hurt with the cold. We shouldn't be here, I kept thinking. I shouldn't be here with her today.

I convinced myself that the pain in the neck, the scalp, the eye was far worse than it had been in the hip, in the leg. It was pain that one saw through: head to scalp to eyes, it was a way of seeing. But perhaps I only thought it was worse because the other pain had gone, and we are incapable of knowing and choosing anything but that which is directly and immediately happening to us.

My fingers ached. I told her how my biggest fear was my fingers. Sylvia would rarely reveal hers, only the time she let me wash her palms, just glimpses when she reached for her coffee cup, the cuff always covering some part of her hands. And so I often wondered, compulsively, if they were damaged by our disease. A little suspicious of her, her covert behaviour. In this sense her body was my biggest fear: the fear of the illness spreading to my hands and fingers. She hid this reality from me, from herself, creating possibility through the unknown.

It seemed I was stuck between the two women. When I went to Frida, Sylvia cried. When I stayed with Sylvia, Frida was angry, told me it was not healthy.

Sylvia stayed with me that day and kept visiting throughout the week. I wanted to say to her, *It's okay, don't come.* I wondered if she made me worse. The pain was worse; fingers, knees, neck. Swollen knuckles, torso feeling like stone.

I walked so as not to hate myself entirely. I woke early most days and walked through the same parks as always, and on better days through to North Melbourne. One morning, as I walked alone, a boy ran in front of me across the footpath. Moments later a kite followed him, dragged along the ground, failing to take flight. Only for a second did the clear angel-hair string emerge in a glint of sun across the path, the silent bouncing kite trailing after him. I halted and tried to smile as he passed, swallowing down the anger. This child with his flying kite seemed to both make and represent the invisible tripwire I expected everywhere. Anxiety and metaphor. *My point*, wrote Sontag, *is that illness is not a metaphor.* And yet there are limited ways to inhabit the body's form of storytelling.

It had been weeks since I'd seen anyone except for Tomasz and Sylvia. My friends asked me to meet them at the bar in Ascot Vale where we'd met just after the operation, the hospital. I explained I wasn't well. The relief, the relief, it was so easy to offer excuses. I was lousy with excuses, full of them, guilty with them, full up with the guilt of them. The sick day—when does it end?

In Sylvia Plath's poem about the plaster woman, a woman lies in bed and feels trapped: there are two of her now. She is her body and she lives with a plaster cast. She is both. The plaster version is supposed to be the one that holds her together, the self presented to the world. At first she is quiet and cold, shaped just the way the woman is shaped. She is subservient, the mould, the face to meet another. And yet she is not the real one; she doesn't even have blood. Eventually the plaster begins to change: she wants to cover the woman entirely, take over her, become her own self completely. Now she, the plaster, looks beyond the body that lies on the bed, to a life she wants. She doesn't fit the body properly anymore. The plaster self wants to leave the body. And yet now the woman is not sure how she will live without the other.

I shall never get out of this! Plath writes about her plaster woman, her situation. And what do we do when our encasing, our casting, our characters don't match the body they mould, the body that casts them? Sylvia in her plaster, the plaster within Sylvia. Do I fashion the symptoms or does the ache manifest me? The skeleton does not make the person.

At the traffic lights, walking home later that week, I couldn't look up properly on account of my neck. But I sensed that someone was near.

'Sylvia.' I said it and wondered if she was there. My voice was cloudy. I wanted to tell her I was nervous, standing there, the road ahead of me. I wanted the lights never to change to green because green meant movement meant pain.

'Isn't it always easier to go nowhere, to not go far?' Her deep, sweet voice.

'I can't look at you properly,' I said. 'I really didn't think I would see you this week. I thought I felt good.'

'I wanted to see you.'

'*I shall never get out of this!*'

'What?'

'Nothing. Do you want to come to mine?'

We went home. We sat on the balcony. Sylvia was in such a good mood. I realised I had been with her for a week straight, maybe longer; she had gone to the park every day, and so had I. She looked out over the bare ginkgos and the London plane trees.

'I want to save something and feed it,' she said. 'A little sad bird. I'll feed it and I'll be its mother. It'll be a creative act. I feel creative today.'

'I feel kind of sick.'

'Me too,' said Sylvia. 'A little of it is necessary.'

'You like the way that sounds,' I accused her. 'Hanging decorations off nausea.'

Sylvia laughed. 'That's beautiful. You made a poem.'

Before she left, Sylvia told me she loved me. She promised me she would come back.

She never seemed to go away. We always sat upstairs. I knew that I was not living as well as I could be. I didn't leave the house often. I made no effort to contact the few friends I had in the city. Some still texted occasionally; did I want to go out to a bar, did I want to have lunch, perhaps a coffee at home? Others had given up. I excused myself from everything. Usually I mentioned my leg, the slow healing, the fatigue, but really it was my neck and my head and my hands, and it was my fear of these things, what they signalled about this body I inhabited, which I saw as a place that was wildly beyond my control. And it was the feeling that I had destroyed the narrative that was expected of me: be sick and in pain, go to hospital, come home and be well. There would always be something else that would cause me pain. This meant, in theory, that I forever had every excuse to cocoon myself away from the world, and that I was dangerously close to living that sort of life for good. Who on earth had I been just a month ago, with Frida, in the salt water, in the chlorinated warmth, in the pools and the sea?

Sylvia allowed all these tendencies in me. She sat with me for long periods of time, right through the morning and into the late afternoon. The sun had passed over the balcony for the day, so we had no choice but to sit in the wake of it.

'Do you want to be with me today?' Sylvia asked late one afternoon, her facial shadows pronounced in the low light. 'Maybe you're sick of me. I understand. But you really do need to rest. And you don't know how to. I don't know if you know this about yourself. I'm trying to help you.'

I didn't answer. She always wanted to sit, up there on the balcony; always to sit and talk. Always searching for some deeper, slightly darker thought.

'Do you want wine?' she asked.

We thought of all the consequences, how sick we would feel, what it would do to our pain, but I did; I said yes, I did.

I felt sick as I started to drink the second glass. I thought of Frida and the pool and how far away she was. I thought of how my absence from the pool was always a significant act. It was an action chosen, an act committed, a threshold crossed. I was frightened by my inclinations towards stagnation and darkness. I was scared that by not going to the pool—it had been some weeks already—I would never go again. I believed wholeheartedly that habits lived on a knife edge.

BODY FRIEND

I slept badly, the alcohol and sugar surging through the body. At three am I drank two glasses of water then lay awake, heart thumping wildly.

A frightened feeling stalked me. I would sit in cafes and try to write, to achieve something in the last week before I was due to go back to the office. My body felt hostile to me, an unwelcome, unfamiliar presence, or perhaps I was the unwelcome presence inside of it. A feeling stalked me; it seemed to insinuate that I did not know what was coming. In public, I was obsessed with finding a seat where nobody was behind me. It was an act of protection, something I adopted after or alongside the neck pain, the headaches and stiff shoulders. Nobody could see me when I could not see them myself. Tomasz, I realised, was not aware of the huge heights and depths I veered between. He was steadfast and present, I remember this, but the ebb and flow of good and bad days was mostly unintelligible to him. If I was in pain, it was to be expected because I had pain that was chronic—a slightly worse day that felt immense to me was not immediately obvious to him. I understood this. Only in the reflections of Frida and Sylvia did I see myself plainly. In front of Tomasz or anyone else, I was a confusion of both or neither.

And then, in the middle of winter, Tomasz went away for a two-day cycling trip. A journey on gravel paths in the deep country. No phone reception, no showers, just campsite meals and dirt roads and campfire soot, their bikes and their bodies and the air. By coincidence our housemate went away too, camping with her girlfriend for the weekend, so I was to be alone for two nights in the house for the first time since the operation.

On a balcony you are released outside but not into freefall. You can see the way back in. I was up there all the time now, even through the winter, sifting through the quiet, catching granules of noise that fell through the walls of the house or travelled up from the street. I wore soft, loose-fitting pants and warm woollen cardigans, thick socks. Before he left, Tomasz had suggested I call my friends and arrange to see them, go to the bar in Ascot Vale as I had done just a few months back, but I got the impression he had no expectation that I would. I heard the neighbours, particularly the loud man who lived next door. If I sat inside at my desk, upstairs in the bedroom, I could hear the sounds of his living room on the other side of the wall. In the hallway, in parts of our living room, I heard faint music coming from the other neighbour's house, gentle piano, and sometimes I put my ear to the wall, leaning against the cool plaster.

I thought of Frida often but had no way of finding a path back to her. The simple confidence I'd once possessed, that ability to get up, ride on a tram, strip off my clothes in the changing rooms and put on bathers in the cold, walk through the foyer, embrace the cold gasp of entering the pool, the weightless turn, the difficult first laps as the body warmed up, all now seemed wondrous to me, a pinnacle from which I'd fallen. The thought of the cold sea repelled me.

Tomasz left early in the morning. He wore his cycling kit and carried only a small bag. He was gone by seven, in the half-light. I tried to go back to sleep, but in what felt like only minutes I heard knocking downstairs.

Sylvia was at the front door.

'You look tired,' she said.

Behind her, a grey morning. Low cloud obscured the houses opposite.

'So do you.'

'We're tired. We haven't stopped in a long time. You haven't stopped, not really, not since the hospital, and that wasn't really stopping anything.'

'The thinking.'

'The thinking doesn't stop. It's tiring,' said Sylvia.

She stayed with me throughout the weekend. Tomasz texted once, from a town he passed through briefly, but mostly he was out of range, high up in the mountains, tracing the gravel roads. We stared at the wall, Sylvia and I; we lay and we stared at the wall, numb and quiet.

We stared at the wall over and over in a very long moment. Two days in a row. We were stone, we were turning into stone. My grinding knees were hot stones. We catnapped in our thick turtleneck jumpers, took painkillers and slept deeply in the soft heat, sweating. When night fell, Sylvia closed all the blinds and I ordered in Thai food. We ate together on the couch downstairs. We were too tired to bathe and so we lay in bed and drank tea and fell asleep early. In the morning I made us coffee in the cold kitchen. Wordlessly, Sylvia got up slowly, sat on the balcony in her dark green jumper, the grey pyjama pants I'd lent her, a pair identical to the ones I wore.

'I shouldn't sleep in bed during the day,' I said. 'I should at least go to the couch downstairs.'

Sylvia laughed. 'A bed is for sleeping. Don't be silly.' She gingerly reached out her hand and I passed her the coffee.

Sylvia convinced me to have more painkillers. To let myself. *Let your body relax some more*, she said. *You're so high-strung with pain. Let your brain rest a little.*

I told her I was worried that if I kept taking them so long after the hospital stay, kept relying on them just to take the edge off, just to have a break from the pain, that I would no longer be me. I worried I would come to depend on them entirely. I would become someone who couldn't function with pain at all, when in fact that very functioning had become me. That was what I knew of me. I was so used to pain that to rely on something to eradicate or pause it would make me unsure where I ended and that other, less pained, painkiller version of me started, nor how much I could cope with; when to relieve it, when to persist. The question of pain and its presence or absence had become a dilemma of identity. On the good days I didn't believe myself, didn't believe the memory of pain, gaslighted myself into shame.

I told Sylvia about the time when, as a child, I went to a friend's birthday party at an indoor ice-skating rink, and the cold sent my body into shock. My vision went blurry, sounds diminished and echoed across the ice. It was the first time I was aware that my body was out of my control. All I wanted was to fall asleep with my head on my arms, on the large wooden steps that formed the stadium seats. My friend's mother noticed, but I refused to acknowledge her, I said nothing.

'Why didn't you say anything?'

I didn't know; I could only guess that it was shame. My body was failing where others weren't. It struck me as highly sensitive; to complain, to mention how I felt. It was only cold, after all. It was only a sensation.

'You should've said something,' said Sylvia.

I told Sylvia that for a long time I wasn't convinced of the need for a diagnosis. What did it achieve, all that naming?

Sylvia looked at me. A doctor had recently suggested a new diagnosis, based on her description of her symptoms. I asked her if she ever got tired of telling them, the doctors and the specialists, about her condition.

'There's always a need to explain. It might be more unsettling when they assume they know your story. When they nod or say that they have seen this, they know this, this is normal, this is common. When that happens, your story loses its singularity. You realise they know it and cannot fix it, but because they have seen it before, these doctors, they assume a kind of mastery over the pain. Your pain and your symptoms, the isolation that you thought was wholly yours, that you might have even had some fondness for, simply because you needed to believe that it meant something—you realise that it is not just yours; it belongs to others. And rather than bringing you comfort, this makes you realise you are simply the sufferer of a disease.'

There had been times, she said, when a doctor acknowledged that her own case of the illness was particularly bad. They showed surprise at the severity of her symptoms, had not seen a case like hers in someone so young. Aggressive, they called it. It was a kind of proof, a sense of corroboration and recognition that she could not bring about simply by talking to them. The body had to be the one to show it. The blood tests, the numbers, those apparently incontrovertible truths—she had a strange relationship with that evidence of her body's self-destruction. *Because that's what we're doing,* she said, *isn't it? We're destroying ourselves.*

When she sat in the doctor's office and heard the numbers and results read out, she felt both betrayed and validated. Her body had those secret ways of communicating that were beyond her control. It spoke to the doctor in a language she did not understand. Yet she was validated because there was accepted evidence; the pain she felt existed in numbers and signs somebody else could read.

I walked downstairs to the kitchen to make us more drinks. 'Something sweet and hot,' she called after me.

I came back upstairs, handed Sylvia a spiced tea with milk and honey.

'What if they do more harm than good?' I asked. 'The medications, all the painkillers.'

'You are obsessed with goodness,' said Sylvia, stirring and stirring her tea. 'There are other ways to be, other contingencies of self.'

We've developed this mechanism called pain to warn us, to alert us to the house fire, to tell us when to run. An immune system confused about what is self and what is foreign is always running outside, screaming, *Fire, fire!*

Even with Tomasz's hand sometimes, his finger inside me, I forget it's good, it's pleasure: pleasure, not pain. But, then, a finger run through a candle flame is enough, is both—and the burn is the breath on skin at night that tells you your lover is breathing.

We lay in bed and stared at the wall and breathed and, when we could, we slept. The weekend dragged on. Two days felt like two weeks. With Sylvia I was fixed in plaster—fragile, secure, muffled, breakable and broken, warm and protected. The smell, a tang of overheated bodies rarely outside, rarely aired. My period came and I bled, warm and heavy, the low pressure in my stomach, my gut bubbled restlessly.

I was sick of Sylvia. She wanted to sit and sleep, or eat and talk, wait for the day to end so we could drink wine and talk in ways we couldn't in the middle of the day. I was always overheated, sitting in the room with her, lying in the bed in our woollen jumpers and cardigans, sitting and sitting in the glaring sun. She wanted to drink hot, sweet drinks and wine, to eat large, rich meals with lots of cheese. I could never say no to her, even if I thought I might not want what she was eating or drinking, or thought that it might make me feel sick.

I would say yes anyway, acquiesce. I could not refuse her and I forgot what it was I really wanted, didn't know if my own want was the same as my body's want; I took these decisions against my body. I didn't listen to it, to whatever quietly urgent messages it may have been sending me through pain and nausea and fatigue. My decisions were made separate from any need the body might have been trying to express.

We stared at the wall, Sylvia and I. My body then was the opposite of my pool body: hair limp, greasy; my stomach too full, always and never hungry; my neck fixed, stuck looking ahead of me; legs turning to stone. We ate sweet, sticky muesli bars, we ate chocolate sweetened with coconut sugar, overripe bananas, tea thick with milk. We were like statues, or women in plaster. Staring and breathing.

But she understood. Sylvia understood so much. She was perhaps as lost as me, but we were so close by then it was difficult to know if she felt the way I did, or if my image of her was a function of my own projections. Sylvia told me she had been thinking of her apartment and how it was so hard to keep it in order lately.

She laughed. 'Dirty towels and wet crumbs on the kitchen counter—why do these things seem to me to be symbols of chaos?'

She told me she lived alone. It had always been too hard to find space for her illness in any relationship. Others were socialised to see the body as they wanted it to be, fixable and predictable, she explained, and it was too much, too great a feat to tell someone all over again, all over again in the body. My disease had gradually revealed itself to Tomasz, perhaps a small mercy; I had let the body slowly show him its ill ways. And yet there would always be great chasms that words couldn't cross. But Sylvia knew, and I could say nothing at all.

We lay still, we stared at the wall. We found it impossible to read. How could we stand a sentence like, *She turned her head*, when it came with no fraught internal dialogue, no suggestion of the exceptionality of the movement? *She turned her head!* A body so able, so unknowable. The inability to comprehend the particular way of being that we knew, Sylvia and me, was an essential failing. A well-known novelist wrote a slim book of essays and in one of them recounted a trip to the massage therapist. She described how the knots in her muscles were relieved and untied; there was a *loosening*, she wrote, a positive, noticeable release in her body. She went to the massage therapist and felt better: the story was almost mythic to us, as fictional as plot, as character. I tried this, of course, going to massage therapists and herbal doctors, each time with the sense that I was kneeling again at the altar of narrative, praying for that good outcome. Imbued in the absence of an ill body is the danger of the normality of such curing metaphors, the falsely able certainty of confirmed narratives, the sure passage from prior pain to a feeling of wellness.

In the past I had followed the online accounts of a video blogger who promoted a so-called healthy lifestyle. Her output charmed me at first: the beautiful mountainous country where she lived, close to a lake; the aesthetically pleasing style of her expensive yet free-for-her ethically made clothes (which, she emphasised, should be consumed slowly and thoughtfully, despite her introducing brand after brand whose products had been given to her at no cost); and the connection to health she seemed to espouse. She exercised diligently but rested consciously. She ate well, those beautifully coloured and crafted bowls, and she ate food that was locally sourced. For a while I found the videos comforting to watch, in an aspirational way. Yet I never let on to Tomasz that I watched them, as though they were a guilty indulgence, and I started to feel uncomfortable with their repetitive narratives. Every few weeks or months she would announce that she had *reset* because her way of living was *just not sustainable*: she was working too much, exercising either too much or not enough, she wasn't eating as regularly or as well as she should be, she was not taking time for rest, not allowing herself to be vulnerable. And the accompanying video would be a remedy for one of those ills: a restful day, an early rise for a swim, a nourishing bowl of food. And the term *self-care* was repeated constantly in this new and good ending to the story, yet it had become so tired and commodified that denouncing it had become the new commodity—any reference to self-care was now prefaced by a denial of any connection to the term as espoused by others, an attempt to distance herself from any beauty or wellness industry speak, or so this blogger said; hers was apparently a different form, self-care without self-care, as if the concept was still acceptable, only the term was not.

Buried somewhere in this ubiquitous concept was a desire to be genuine about caring for the body, but the need to recount a clear and linear narrative, rather than the boring, essential rhythm of our bodies, had stripped the term of anything useful or accessible for a person who really did want to know how on earth to *look after themselves*. Each of the blogger's videos seemed a remedy for ills that were never apparent in any of the earlier ones. They never showed the moments of her falling into those unsustainable habits, any moment of crisis or hint of unhappiness. Each narrative was the same: a problem identified at the moment of its panacea's arrival, uttered only in the past tense. Good outcome after good outcome. *I was this, but, thank goodness, I am now that.* I had seen this narrative in several others' stories, even in the online accounts of people I knew. They bothered us, these narratives. We knew no stories so unequivocal.

We lay still, staring at the wall. We remained inside. Sylvia stayed through the nights Tomasz was away, through the second night when I barely slept, turning over in pain, through four in the morning and the call of birds in the five o'clock blue. I loved and hated that early hour I'd been gifted by pain. The quiet, drained colour, the first awareness of others waking, a tram bell at the stop on Royal Parade, the first early cars pulling out of driveways in a brief flare of headlights. Sylvia sat up with me, alert and quiet. As dawn broke I drifted off; she'd dissolved aspirin for me in a glass of water, its gentle hiss as soothing as a voice. As other people rose to meet the day, the weekend, we retreated, Sylvia and me, and we slept.

I woke later and it was light. Sylvia and I had been inside for two days. She sat at my desk, looking out the window, as quiet as a cat.

'Did we sleep?'

'Some.'

She walked over and handed me a glass of water, two tablets. We lay in bed. Perhaps Frida had been too harsh on me, on us. My mouth thick and warm, I said, 'Sylvia, I thought I had to be good all the time. We are attacking ourselves, with our bodies; we do the bad and so we must also be the good.'

'Good, bad, good, bad, me and you, you and me.' Sylvia's voice rose and fell like a song. 'There are more than just twos, you know.' She touched my forehead, which felt warm, or her fingers felt warm. She tucked my hair behind my ear.

When the tablets kicked in we went downstairs to make coffee.

'Today I have to go,' she said. 'He'll be home soon; you will pick up a bit.'

She took me back upstairs to bed and I dozed, and when I woke she was gone, as if she had been an apparition all along.

When Tomasz did come home, it was earlier than I'd expected, before I'd had sufficient time to ready myself: get dressed, shower, take more painkillers. Instead, he found me staring at the wall, as I had been for hours, days. He said my name and dropped his bag at the same time. He crossed the room quickly. I could smell earth and sweat.

'What's wrong? What's happened?' His face was dirty and sun-tanned.

'Oh, it's nothing. Sylvia was here.' I must have tried to smile.

'Have you been in bed all weekend?'

I shrugged. 'Sylvia said I needed to rest.'

He came over to the bed and pulled me up into his arms. I knew that this scared him, the notion of giving up, giving in: the perhaps unforgiveable acquiescence.

'I haven't given up,' I said.

He shook his head. 'What are you saying? Let's get you into the shower.'

And he did: he ran the water and took off my t-shirt and pyjama pants, underwear with a blood-soaked pad stuck to it. I didn't even care; didn't care that my clothes smelled overworn, damp and sweet. He stood by the shower door and told me about his weekend, the sights and the campfires. He held the towel as I stepped out of the shower and he helped me dress. We walked through the university to Carlton, and I was dizzy with the air and movement. We ate dinner outside, as we did a lot then, sitting beneath the restaurant gas heaters, on the street-side chairs under the London plane trees. He didn't say anything more about the condition he'd found me in, and I didn't know if I loved or resented him for this. There are gentle and loving ways of ignoring, just as there are of acknowledging. This is one of those little struggles, I realised, when we're cognisant of stagnation or movement on a spectrum of awareness, attention, recognition, ignorance, disregard, boredom, wilful forgetting—experienced with each person, each lover, each stranger, boss, colleague, doctor, waiter, lifeguard, hairdresser, friend.

The next week I left the house to go to the Chinese doctor. Tomasz had insisted I try something for the pain. My body lay sweat-slicked, neck sticky with tiger balm, in front of the doctor who didn't ask me questions, just asked for my body: show me your tongue; give me your wrist so I can take your pulse; look me in the eye. I liked him. I liked that my body was the one to show him what was wrong. The Western doctors were obsessed with story, and wanted to listen to the body through words that didn't appear to tell them anything if those words did not already confirm what was expected of the condition, or through numbers that cast a pall over the line between physiology and feeling.

The doctor wore a neat blue suit over his wide body, his stomach pressing uncomfortably at his shirt. *I eat too much red meat*, he said. It caused him to have a lot of anger, he explained. *I need to eat less*, he said. He laughed. *Maybe I can give you some of my fat.* He practised from a low-fronted shop on a busy street in Footscray, full of bakeries and discount shops. Next door to his clinic was a hair salon that played loud hip-hop music from early in the morning. He put needles into my knees, feet, jaw, forehead and left me to lie, palms up, for forty minutes. I asked him, how long might it take? To fix me?

'It will take time—Rome wasn't built in a day,' he said, then chuckled, as though he liked the sound of the phrase.

The treatment rooms were the size of a bed plus a little more, divided only by curtains, rooms separated by little more than air and cotton, little more than the skin of our eyelids and, not unlike the hospital, I could hear everything happening in the beds on either side of mine. Most people went through the hour of their appointment in near silence. Occasionally somebody was very loud. A woman moaned and called out sharply. She breathed heavily and kept repeating, *I'm so sore, aren't I, ow ow ow ow. I'm so tight, aren't I?*

Another time, at a massage clinic in the city, a man in the space next to me spoke throughout his entire treatment. He asked the therapist how bad it was, said that he had been told he had the tightest, most painful knots that other massage therapists had ever encountered. He sounded proud of it. The woman treating him responded with a polite murmur; she seemed very young. Most of the women and men working there were young, some of them barely twenty years old, from China, from Thailand, working eleven-hour days, encompassing with their hands the bodies of these white men and women who were twenty, fifty, sixty, who wanted announcement and recognition of their pain. The young woman murmured, *Yes, it's very tight*, said it several times, and this seemed to placate the man, who wanted the verbal validation of his pain. He thanked her several times as he left. I liked hearing the young women whisper and laugh together between clients, felt relieved for them to have those moments in between all of us. For several months, I returned to one of those clinics in the city to see the same massage therapist, a young man who seemed to find my pain in ways others could not. One day he wasn't there. He'd gone to work in a factory, one of the other young men told me, and I felt an unaccountable loss at his absence; perhaps I even missed him for a while.

In those treatments I always stayed silent. Mostly I hated the fact that an overt display of suffering appeared to be the only way to validate or express it. Through the progression of the disease I'd developed a perception that deep pain was relative to the silence it brought. Some belief in chronic pain's capacity to destroy expression, even the groan, even the shout. Perhaps I was just stubborn, unreasonably proud of my silence.

I arrived home from the clinic feeling thirsty and a heady kind of exhaustion. I always wanted to sleep after these appointments. I told Tomasz that I went because I was sore—always feeling the need to justify the cost, the perceived extravagance associated with the word *massage*, or I'd emphasise *acupuncture*, as though it were more akin to treatment than rest or relaxation. Of course, he didn't care what I spent my money on and always said it was a good thing if I had a treatment. And yet every time I went, I would say to him: *I was hurting more than usual today, I thought it would help.*

Tomasz had cycled some hundred or so kilometres that day, had ridden up and then down a mountain. He was exhausted and happy.

'I don't want to do *anything*,' he said, sighing, stretching out on the bed. He'd just showered, put on a fresh t-shirt and boxer shorts. His cheeks were pink from sun and exertion. I lay down next to him, put a hand on his chest. His heartbeat was slow and measured. 'Let's order in food,' he said.

'I don't mind cooking; I've spent enough money today.'

'I'll get it. It's *Saturday*, we don't need to cook.'

I was so thankful for his sureness in moments like this. A reminder that there was not always a vague moral debt to pay, that it was okay to shrug and sigh and say, *I don't want to do anything,* just as easily as he could say, *We're fine, we can order in if we feel like it.* We understood each other's anxieties around money, had both grown up with the tension born of scarcity, the looks between parents and the frustration and fights that only ever seemed to be about money and which made us both feel, with the reductive purity of childhood reasoning, that our parents would've been a hundred per cent happy if they did not have to worry about money. Tomasz understood that I could never quite forgive myself for spending what seemed to be exorbitant amounts on my body and its health supplements or herbs or apparent fixes that were not absolutely essential, but which gave me at least a measure of hope or sense of control.

'What are you thinking about?' said Tomasz.

'I don't know. What food do you want?'

'Thai? It's always good. And they're so nice.'

'I love that you can make decisions so easily. It's a very lovable quality. We could walk down.'

He shrugged. 'A walk would be good.'

I returned to work. I worked at the office job once a week, taught at the university, kept up with my research and writing. I was shocked by how everything was exactly the same in the office and on campus, right down to the position of each colleague's coffee cup on the shelf, even the stained one that nobody used; the greetings each person said and the small talk I entered into with them; the place I sat for lunch and the places the other employees preferred to sit and eat their lunch; the days of the week they worked and when they took their breaks, some eating so early it was barely midday, others chewing at their desks into the afternoon.

People asked a predictable range of questions. How was I feeling? Was I all better now? I must feel like a new person, they said. For the most part I said much better, thanks, or that recovery was slow but I was feeling good. Never did I try to pull them down into any uncomfortable truths of incurability. I went along with the simpler, easier, before-and-after story.

And in some moments this story was true, while in others it wasn't. It is as if I exist in the photograph called *Double Portrait* by Dora Maar. Two faces of the same woman are joined, overlapping precisely where one ends and the other begins, to create one face in doubled form. One woman looks ahead and upwards; the other is in profile. I interpret her as two manifestations of the same person: one half is in pain while the other half feels perfectly well. Having sex I am a divided double portrait; my body wants and wants and moves, and the other half, from my neck to scalp and down to the spine, flits and flinches at the pain. The moment of orgasm is the most split between pleasure and pain I've ever been, the incision of feeling into self at its absolute form. Is this some miraculous philosophy attained? It feels so rotten, so true, so indicative of other moments, daily moments I've lived through but in which I haven't been so aware of the division.

Perhaps in these lesser moments the split between pleasure and pain manifested in a sense of fragmentation in desire. In such moments I went out and did nice things, lunches, drinks at bars, and I smiled, smiled quite genuinely, but another part of me experienced it completely differently and I resented where I was. My head and neck might be taut and throbbing, the increasing sensation like rising noise levels. Or in moments of Tomasz seeming in awe of my body, touching my body, pressing my breasts together and kissing the pushed-up flesh of them, wanting it more and more it seemed, while I was aware of my body's illness, otherness, its capacity to destroy itself. Fulfilment and contentment existed with a veil of pain; joy as real as the ache. This was entirely possible and it happened all the time. I had realised this, but it didn't seem to mean much to say it to anyone. Our fantastic magnitudes are ours alone.

I went to the City Baths again, but only because I hoped to see Frida. More than a month had passed since I'd been to the pool, since I'd seen her or been in the water. I was ashamed of it. The water mocked me; I realised it didn't need me. I'd constructed my relationship with it and I could very well tear it to pieces. Frida was the water, she was my relationship to it, I wanted them both and yet in other moments I despised them. I could have told her I was scared—yes, scared—of the new pain and aberrant movements in my skull and neck, signifiers of new problems, yet the admission of fear made it seem unworthy of her, no excuse at all.

We stood outside the changing room, an unsettlingly liminal and cold place, Frida in her bathers, her hair in a cap. I said to Frida that I was only watching that day. I told her that I hoped we could have coffee. Her expression appeared neutral. My neck wouldn't move properly, I explained, almost pleading, and the headache had a fogging effect on my senses. I'm not sleeping, I told her.

'It's not an excuse,' I said.

'Don't come,' she said. 'Don't come if you won't swim.'

'I wanted to see the water. I wanted to know what is possible.' I wanted to know who I wished to be.

She walked away into the main pool area. She swam fast, and for a long time, stayed there in the water for an hour. I sat on a bench, feeling nauseous in the fuggy, chlorinated air. I imagined her fingers, my fingers, gone soft, pink-wrinkled by the water.

She took her time getting dressed.

'You're addicted to your other friend,' she said. 'Sylvia.'

'You're jealous.'

Frida scoffed. 'Why didn't you just swim? You came all the way here.'

'It's my neck. It's no good.' I was scared, I told Frida, because it was, this is, an ebb-and-flow disease, cyclical yet unintelligible, because I didn't know where I was in the cycle, how long each turn would be, what the next would entail, how that day I thought it would be my neck that went bad next, the grinding, cracking, stiffening, words words words, the fear of it.

'You're letting the fear control your actions, the disease control your thoughts. Swim with me, you will feel better,' said Frida. She paused. 'Why wouldn't you want to feel better?'

There is a pain point, I told her, that makes it feel impossible.

She said something about how pain is always the same, the going or not going to the pool was just related to how I felt about it. My behaviour, she said, my action or inaction, was connected only to how I felt about the pain that day. I was in a precarious position, she warned. If I stopped swimming there was no certainty I'd ever return. She was imperious and it seemed wonderful to me; I was in awe of her devotion to the pool.

I tried the next day. I put on my bathers, my new ones, the colour called ox blood, the brand name in white lettering, and my purple swimming cap. It hurt to put on the cap: the pain was in my neck and scalp and the tops of my shoulders, and in my head I was naming, naming, naming. I knew Frida was next to me, I could see her in the mirror but I couldn't turn my head properly to look at her. I'd have to turn my whole body and that would make me unsteady on my legs.

'I'm no good today,' I said. 'My body's no good.'

'You'll be in the water soon,' she said. For the first time her voice was almost soothing, it nearly soothed me. I looked ahead at the two of us in the mirror. And when her voice echoed a little in the changing room I thought I might have been the one talking. *Remember the water.* She said things like this. I repeated these phrases to myself later and they sounded unreal, even trite. They had a particular quality when Frida said them.

We walked the distance from the changing room to the foyer to the pool. My days were made of such distances. The cold shower, the cold skin, the cold chest, the cold gasp of entering the pool. All of it both familiar and strange. Feelings and sensations both numbed and heightened by pain.

There was a mother and child near me, and a man in his thirties floating on his back. Their closeness made me anxious, made me nearly angry, close to anger and close to crying. I dropped my body down into the water and under the lane rope, into the slow lane. Frida was already ahead, swimming. I followed her, struggled to turn my neck to the side, I swallowed some water and I wondered, too, if there was someone behind me or close by me and whether they would knock into me or if I would make them angry because I was slow. This was the fear, really: that I was in trouble in some way—a strange guilt, a hypervigilance and fear, and it was all in the mind and all in the body.

Frida didn't notice, or didn't acknowledge, my anxious state. I wasn't sure if this was a kindness or neglect. I soon got out of the water.

I knew she was disappointed in me. At the pool entrance we walked down the steps together but we didn't go for coffee. She didn't suggest it and I didn't want to go with her. It was a bad experience, that was a bad experience: I repeated this to myself on the tram home. A bad pool experience. The words hung in my mind throughout the evening, through dinner with Tomasz and as we lay in bed watching a film, and they continued to ring out as I drifted towards sleep.

I worked the next day. I thought of Frida. Throughout the day—at my desk, in the lunch room, during conversations with people—I felt on a pendulum between two different selves. One could not quite break through into the day of others or shake the desire to be alone, unsettled when a colleague approached me with a question, recoiling inside when I passed a familiar face on the campus, wanting to be at home with my thoughts. The other self controlled the illness, or at least how she felt about it; she was a more clear and confident person who could move easily through rooms, swim after work, speak with a steady voice. And sometimes I longed for certitude or permanence, that one of the selves might triumph.

An email came through from human resources, with links to various videos on the Health Channel. I put headphones on and listened to a video narrated by a psychologist, a woman with dark hair and a polished New Zealand accent, golden jewellery and dressed in black. Her dialogue—which I thought must have been scripted, though it came across as natural and spontaneous—was far more resonant and deep than I'd expected. I listened to every word and then listened to it again.

If we actually knew the real power of the mind, she said, we would be petrified of what we allowed in. We didn't let thieves come and just ransack our homes for our valuables, did we? So why let thuggish thoughts into our minds? Her voice became almost indignant. We needed a guard, she said: a gatekeeper to stop them. From the Bible to self-help books, we were reminded that whatever you thought you were, whatever you put after the words *I am*, that's what you were, that's what your life was. But we filtered and personalised what we heard about ourselves and what we said to ourselves. We were subjective to the point of danger. We polarised: every thought and experience was either good or bad. And so, if we did not meet the high, even unreasonable standards we set for ourselves, we automatically let the thuggish, negative thoughts in. She then recommended ways to stop the negative thoughts from entering and taking root: consciously replacing one negative thought with two positive ones, maintaining gratitude as an antidote to fear, among other things. And *exercise*, the psychologist implored. Exercise, because in those moments you could not be in your mind and your body at the same time.

In those strange and difficult days after returning to work, I thought of Frida so often I was ashamed. It was as if she set the course for how a life should be lived, and if I didn't stay close to her, in the water, in my mind, in action and thought, I would forget her example and go about my routines in entirely the wrong way, until they became habits. Until they became the person I was.

I tried so hard to stay close to Frida, even though I thought she might have been getting sick of me. She never wanted to hear an excuse. I was only good if I swam with her in the pool. She held me to this standard, insisted that I meet this expectation, and I was in thrall to it when I felt able, terrified of it when the pain was bad. She said when I didn't swim, she felt as though I'd rejected her. Sometimes it was as if, silently, viscerally, we detested as much as we loved each other. The dependence on one another. A very internal kind of hatred and love. It was in the scalp, in the muscles; we never said a word about it.

The air was warm and salty at the Sea Baths, with less of the suffocating chlorine of the city pools. I was sure Frida would be there. In the hydrotherapy spa I saw the usual group of older bathers, the couples with thin or bulging bodies, the man with the sinewy, wrinkled limbs and chest, a silver chain around his neck, who floated by himself but always stopped by the group for a few words before leaving the warm pool. It was winter and the windows facing the sea were fogged over in a murky patchwork. Despite the cold, a few people went out through the opaque door onto the sand. Some put on neoprene socks and caps, others went barefoot. When they exited, as though crossing an elemental barrier from solid mass to mist to liquid, each wore an expression of calm focus. I never seemed to see anyone come back inside.

From the hydrotherapy pool, I looked over to the lap pool on the other side of the room. In one of the lanes, swimming by herself, I saw Frida. She paused at the end of the lane and took off her goggles. She saw me and beckoned me over.

    I went into the lane where she waited, breathing, her face bright, dripping gently with water. I swam, following her. At times, with the lenses of the goggles fogging, my head unable to turn very far in breathing, my neck unable to lift my head up to look ahead of me, Frida disappeared from sight completely. She simply wasn't there in the lane with me. I thought she might have left, but then a pane of her leg would appear under the water; a wash of skin, pale olive, would emerge through the warm and hazy blue; or I would feel her current stream past me and know that I'd just missed her.

I've thought often since of her capacity to disappear like that, to make me feel that she existed just beyond my perception.

We went for coffee afterwards, as we so often had before. We were calm, and I was relieved. We sat outside, by the shore. The weather had put most people off, but Frida insisted on it. She wanted the air, she said; she needed it. I loved that about Frida. It would have been so easy to say that it was too cold, too windy, too something, and to seek what we thought was comfort, but she was always adamant that resisting the weather, the seasons, would rob us of a deeper sensation beyond comfort that might even approach happiness.

Sitting outside on that fitful, windy day, beneath grey skies, I was aware that my skin felt everything through Frida, everything through a brain that was in an encounter with her, my encounter with her, so that I wondered whether I'd ever really felt anything just as it was, raw, or whether I only felt things through the day's mood, through the people I sat with, the body's level of pain, and whether all those various determinants made the way I felt any less real.

Frida said that she often overheard people, mostly women—in clothes shops or in cafes, in trains or walking past, talking on their phones—say things like, *I just don't have any self-control; I need to get better at controlling myself.* They planned to attain that control in the near future. *Once I'm on leave from work, I'll get myself sorted; I'll exercise, I'll eat better. Starting next week, I'll look after myself.* Frida confessed to what she called an ugly judgement she felt towards them. She thought that they should just start being better *now*, that they were weak-willed, that they owed their body more than to hurt it, to disrespect it even. She conceded that this was no doubt linked to the parts of herself she judged in harsh ways, and what she might have done better in her own past, towards her own body: her fussy eating as a child, the junk food she ate as a teenager, how she drank too much in her early twenties and then, by twenty-five, was sick enough to know control was paramount, even if impossible. We felt many of the same things. There was great power in believing we were in control of how we felt, of how our bodies were.

I loved Frida because she had the necessary control, she was so good, it seemed, she was so right about things. And I wanted what she had: the discipline and the virtue that accompanied it.

After a few more days in her company, I was back in alignment with Frida. The confidence I felt when I had Frida in my head and body stayed with me even on the days I didn't see her. She was there, inhabiting me somehow, through the skin of my arms, my chest. Standing in the shower, a feeling of contentment and zealousness. Me, smiling, humming, bending down easily. Sex was easy and good. I was far from my mind. It was exactly what made me happy. The simplistic love of a dog towards myself and my body. I heard Tomasz telling his mother that I was a lot better, so much better. I was confirming the narrative. I did not intervene to complicate it.

It would have been easy to say that I needed both of them: that the relentless physicality of Frida pushed me into the languishing state that was being with Sylvia; that the fog-and-stone feeling that came over me on the days I spent with Sylvia was a necessary pause which, being tolerable for only a limited amount of time, drove me to seek the movement and cold of the pool with Frida. The only conclusion I would have been certain of at the time was that such formulations would have felt like an intolerable violence to me, a piercing and pinning down of story and logic, narrative and symbolism, when none of it resembled what it felt like.

I didn't see Sylvia for the rest of the winter. I worked most days, either teaching or at the office or on my thesis and writing. In the spring, the Carlton Baths reopened and I recognised the people I'd seen back in summer and early autumn. I started to swim outside again.

One day, coming home from work, I went to the City Baths, as it was close to my tram stop going home. It still surprised me that I did things like this, that I had the energy and capacity for them.

Frida was already in the pool. I noticed straightaway that something wasn't right. She didn't move her head easily. She made little eye contact. It was as if she didn't want to be with me, didn't want to be in the pool, as though she was in pain. She got out of the water after only a short swim. I, on the other hand, wanted to swim for hours. That was my mood, how I felt. Still accustomed to following her, I got out of the pool and went with Frida to the changing rooms. She walked with her body bent forwards, the weight and pressure all on her left leg, while her right leg appeared shorter, bent awkwardly. It gave her body a strange sense of asymmetry.

'Frida,' I said.

As I tried to reach out to her, she recoiled.

'I feel like resting,' she snapped. 'Are you happy?'

We knew angry pain well, the viciousness and immediacy of it, the way it made you detest the ones you loved most.

'I think I hate you today,' she said. 'I hate everyone today. I feel angry.'

'You need to get an X-ray,' I said. 'The leg.'

'I know. You know too much about this.' She shook her head as she spoke.

On the steps of the City Baths we felt a light breeze. Frida stood and closed her eyes for a moment. Trams sailed past, going to and from the universities in the city and further north in Carlton. A man in gym clothes, holding a large drink bottle, stepped around us and into the building.

'Let's get a drink and just rest for a while,' I said.

'I should keep going.'

'It's okay to stop sometimes.'

She laughed in a bitter way. 'Is it just? Haven't I told you about the stopping: the danger of it, the never-coming-back from it? Don't you know what hangs over every minute of my life?'

'Just here.' I pointed to the cafe beneath the steps of the red-brick building. 'You're anxious, I know. The walking.'

'It's the walking, I'm anxious.'
'I know.'
'It's my leg,' she said.
'If you name the place, does it help?'
'Of course not,' she snapped.
'Of course it does.'

As we made our way down the staircase, Frida let me hold her by the elbow. I had not anticipated Frida's decline. In truth, I feared it, for the heights and depths it suggested, a limitless potential for suffering in the body.

'It's okay to be angry,' I said.
'We didn't ask for this.'
'We didn't ask for this and it's okay to be angry.'

In the days and weeks that followed, Frida agreed when I suggested we swim. *It can't hurt*, I said. *It can't hurt us*, she said. It couldn't hurt, we reasoned, though Frida found it difficult to walk from room to room; she held on to chair backs, tables, walls. If I tried to help her make the tea, she got angry. *I can pick up a teacup, for god's sake.*

Frida said the pain felt material, structural, a stone-like scraping, abraded bones.

'I don't know why I try to describe it to you,' said Frida. She said things like that. *I don't know what saying that achieves*, she'd say with a sarcastic laugh. *I sound ridiculous.* She spoke about her own words with a sort of loathing that was abrupt, shocking.

'As soon as I say these things, I hate them,' she said. 'They close me off from how it really feels. It just feels . . .' She shrugged, sniffed, and said no more.

We walked slowly to the Sea Baths. It was September and a few spring days in those later weeks of the month were warm, even hot. From then on we went only to the Sea Baths or the sea itself. Frida wasn't able to travel far, to swim in the city or in Carlton. She seemed apologetic, said she was furious she couldn't do it, wondered whether she really could but was letting her thoughts get the better of her. At this time I thought I might be getting stronger—not better; this was a story I'd stopped believing in and rather had found other possibilities, other story arcs of the body. Yet in Frida's decline there was something abject, something frightening in its suggestive reality.

She stopped swimming laps at all and simply floated in the sea or the pool.

Frida no longer loved the open water. 'I'm just too scared. It's my leg, my knees, it's the illness telling me what to do and what I can't do,' she said.

I often encouraged, or pushed her, to come outside to the sea. *You're okay*, I said. *How do you know?* she asked, as though desperate. I thought I might be getting stronger because of the way I perceived the open water, the way I acted before it. I faced it. I did not fear the cold. I walked to meet the sea with calm. There was no dread of the body being pulled from one state to another, from clothed to near naked, from temperate to freezing. I was barely thinking of my swollen knees or my hips or the stiffness in my neck. They were all present, all those pains, but they seemed to stop a certain distance from the edges of my mind.

Meanwhile Frida moved her legs in an almost mulish way, resistant, as though putting her body through this took the whole force of her will and discipline.

Frida said: 'My skin has an inner lining and today I call it anger. Synovial fluid has an egg white-like consistency, did you know this? My sick, ugly leg. It hardens, it's a slow wound, and then you carry around these knees.'

'We both have these knees,' I said.

'We carry them around.'

Frida refused painkillers, though I tried to convince her. She thought she was hiding the truth if she did not meet the pain in its fullness. Every now and then she would shrug, throw her hands up and say, *Can we just stop talking about it?*

I convinced her to take the lightest dose of paracetamol. She chewed them with her back teeth, her jaw grinding. Frida seemed to respond to a certain sternness, a strict voice that might have echoed the internal voice she knew I also possessed while at pains to cultivate an external appearance of calm.

Watching Frida in pain was not the same as seeing other people in pain. I've said this. I knew the pain but did not feel sorry or sad for her—it was as though I thought with her, this woman I both knew and barely knew. Her hesitations and fears and her ruthless pursuit of working with the body, and in doing so overcoming its power to control, were also mine.

I knew nobody else who knew Frida. Nobody had seen me with her. When you know someone in such limited circumstances, the person you are with them is amplified. You become more faithful to that part of yourself.

If Tomasz had suddenly appeared, if he and Frida and me were all abruptly in the same room, meeting each other eye to eye, face to face, words to words, I had no idea who I would be before them.

I'd seen Tomasz in pain a few times. Once, it was his tooth, the nerve was inflamed, the tooth infected, and he felt pain in his head and neck, down one side of his body. He lay next to me in our room upstairs in the share house, the room with the balcony, and we watched a TV show. Soon he rolled over, mumbled that he couldn't, he didn't want to; there was something childlike about it. He seemed bothered by noise. His ability to take in any external stimuli had shut down. It was a small revelation, to see what pain could do. To witness that and wonder what effect, warped and spreading over conscious experience, this could have on a person in a protracted state, the notion of chronic pain as a frequency only you can hear.

We sat in Frida's apartment. It was dim and blue. Frida had been to the doctor in the afternoon.

'It's gone bad again,' she said. 'My leg, my hip bone.' Frida told me, as though confessing, that five years earlier she'd had the same surgery, the same procedure, that I'd had just months ago.

'I'm supposed to be better now. I was like this before . . .' She spread her palms as if to say here, in the body, inside this. 'I was like this before. Tell me what you were like before.'

'I was like this,' I said, gesturing to her, to me. Here, in the body, this.

'So what's going to happen then?'

I didn't know, of course.

I insisted she let me order in food for her. Frida said I should join her, probably she wanted me to, but I'd been due to meet Tomasz nearly an hour ago.

'Are you seeing your other friend?' Frida tried to shift away from me. She found the movement difficult. I could barely see her. She finally turned the lamp on. 'Go then,' she said.

'I'll visit again soon,' I said, touching her shoulder lightly.

She stared out beyond the balcony at the view that did not take in the sea.

I met Tomasz and his friends in the city. Siglo Bar had a partially covered rooftop terrace with views of the government buildings across Spring Street. I could not quite believe I had made it there. All those stairs. From the body that had been, just a year ago. It felt almost disloyal, to be living like this now. As if I didn't have a care or didn't reckon with pain anymore. As if I was acting, dressed up in a costume or disguise, playing somebody I was not but wanted to be. I told Tomasz how Frida and I would sit below this very venue, outside the European cafe three floors below. In the days just after the surgery, when we walked slowly from the hydro-therapy pool. For me this had more importance than I could convey. He nodded and sipped his beer, cupped my head in his hand for a moment, tucked my hair behind my ear.

It was twenty-three degrees, people wore t-shirts or singlets or thin dresses, the night was a long pink sentence with a pleasant cadence that stops just when it should. Occasionally, putrid cigar smoke drifted towards us, usually sent by a thickset man in a business suit. The stretching dusk continued in ever-dimming orange and grapefruit light.

I took a train to St Kilda before light. It was strange to be going to Frida's apartment, going so early and yet not to the pool. We were not going that day. I barely knew her without the pool. Frida had stopped swimming. She mostly lay in bed at home, or took copious amounts of painkillers if she had to go to the university to work, trying to hide the obvious limp. *I hate it*, she said, *I hate the way I walk*. She told me she had baths every night now, that she liked to let the weightless warmth hold her body.

Frida sat on the sofa near the window. She said my name.

'I just want to sit today,' she said, sighing, dropping her head to her chest. She was buried in warm clothes, in a large woollen jumper, old green cashmere, loose jeans and black shoes. I couldn't see any of her body. Not her legs or her neck or her arms, hands, shoulders. In the pool she was all body, we were all body. But at that moment, I couldn't see her. Frida's cat lay curled up asleep at the other end of the sofa.

'Are you ready?'

Frida nodded almost sulkily. Her personality now was not what I was used to. I was accustomed to her strong voice and steady breath. Frida had no steadiness that day. She put her hand out, wrapped her fingers around my arm. I saw her wrist, a little of the skin of her arm.

We got into the taxi. It was so early there was barely a sound on the street. There was barely light. The air was salt-laced. Always the suggestion of the sea. Frida's soft breathing was the only noise; it took up the space around us. The sky was an image developing, morning emerging from the black.

Sitting in the back of the taxi, we were identical and quiet. We faced ahead, hands in our laps. I looked over at Frida and saw her looking ahead, looking just like me. She looked just like me. Side on. Hair in the dark. I felt things for her that I felt for myself and I wanted to comfort her, us, both.

She looked over at me.

'It's so quiet,' she said. 'Everywhere.'

I told her that when I had my first surgery, on my left knee, when I was twenty-two, I had to wake up in the dark. I was living with my parents then, in the cold blue town beneath the mountain, so it was a long drive into the city.

In the dark, we got into the car. My mother, my father, and me. My father drove.

Frida sighed. 'Maybe I would like that. To be a girl with my mother again.' Frida looked ahead. The daylight grew. Her face, my hands, the driver's profile, emerged.

Frida told me that the doctor had warned her the revision surgery was complex, with more potential for things to go wrong than a regular joint replacement operation. In the early morning quiet we sat under the fluorescent lights of the waiting area. Frida had changed into a thin white hospital gown. Her feet were bare.

Frida leaned in close to my shoulder and whispered, 'I want to call out, *I was just here! I was just here!* I'll sound ridiculous.'

I held her hand as she breathed.

I walked around Richmond while I waited for a call from the hospital. Frida said she didn't want to bother her family with the surgery; they lived interstate, it was easier not to tell them these things. She asked if I'd act as her person: *The one they call, you know, when it's done.*

She was to stay in the hospital for five days. During the first afternoon I sat next to Frida while she slept or, as she did sometimes, lay with her eyes open, looking at me from time to time, blinking, not speaking. I went home for the night and came back the next day. Frida was still in the hospital gown, sitting upright in bed. The nurse had suggested she take a shower. Frida told me this in a voice that seemed panicky.

'I don't know if I can,' she said, looking at me.

'I'll help. I'll help wash you.'

She gripped my arm as we walked the short distance from the hospital bed to the bathroom with the wide shower, the metal bars, and linoleum flooring. Frida held a metal bar while I helped her out of the gown. Her breaths were sporadic and sharp when they came. The contours of her swollen limbs reminded me of my own: the knees, elbow, even the patched hip. Fine goosebumps stippled her breasts and arms. I ran the shower, careful to test the water temperature, pulling up the sleeves of my shirt to run the lukewarm water over my arm. Frida slowly pulled off her underwear, one taut breath after another. *Shit, it's caught.* As I helped her manoeuvre them over the wound site, she laughed once—*Sorry, this is gross*—but the dried trail of discharge, the soft crumpled material, was simply familiar to me, simply evidence of a body like mine.

As the room began to fill with steam I remembered myself in high school, spending a night at a friend's house, and waking to see her blood-filled tampon on the bedroom floor. She had pulled it out in the night and, clearly too tired to get up, had let it soak into the small rectangular rug on the floor. I recalled a sense of disgust, feeling that she was too close, my friend, her body was too much, which might have been equivalent to being too externalised, exposed. The world expected the body to be reined in, the internal hidden; my friend's unthinking, free act broke every rule of control. It was different with Frida. It was seeing my own body.

Frida stood under the warm water and gave a tired smile. 'Water again,' she said in a soft voice.

I held her arm as she got into bed. Frida lay back and closed her eyes. I picked up my phone, sent a message to Tomasz to say that I would be home late, to have dinner without me, not to wait up. From the bed, Frida watched me with sleepy, glassy eyes.

'Do you want anything?' I asked.

Frida yawned. 'You know, I'd love a muesli bar. Something sweet. I can't do another fish-and-vegetables dinner.'

'I'll go now,' I said.

On the street outside the hospital, the air was warm and clear. Late afternoon. I exited onto a quiet back street, walked to the main road with its convenience stores and tram stops. In that beautiful air, I noticed the ease of my steps, the near-absence of pain. It's the thought process I recall—registering to myself that I couldn't really feel pain at that moment, how this matched the warmth and calm of the day—rather than any sense of what that felt like in my body; perhaps, like pain itself, its absence is also difficult to remember.

I found a small metro supermarket on the map on my phone and walked towards it. For some reason I seemed to be walking against the direction of foot traffic, and had to dodge people to avoid them touching me. A short distance ahead a woman stood in the middle of the footpath, causing people to walk around her or stop abruptly before continuing on. As I got closer I realised it was Sylvia, though this seemed an almost impossible sight.

'Hi,' she said. Her voice rang clear.

'Sylvia. Hi.' I felt sure I had made a mistake, that I'd called her by the wrong name. I was with Frida today. It was like being found out, guilty, betraying someone, committing some wrongful act. It was transgressive, the feeling, as if I'd caused a seeping of the compartmentalised parts of myself.

'What are you doing here?' It seemed so silly, once I'd said it.

'I had an appointment,' said Sylvia, waving her arm vaguely towards the street, where there were several specialists and a radiology department in the vicinity of the hospital. 'I haven't seen you in the park for so long.'

I may have looked behind me then. For reasons I couldn't explain, I worried Frida would suddenly appear and I would have to confront the two of them, my two friends, together in one place. I told Sylvia that I'd had less time lately, since returning to work. I spent long days at the computer now, or else had to travel to the campus a few times a week.

'I'll see you in the park again soon,' I said. 'Maybe on the weekend.'

'All right then,' said Sylvia. A pause. 'I haven't seen you in such a long time.'

'It's been nice to be busy,' I said.

Sylvia nodded. 'As long as you are feeling good. It's not essential, you know, to be busy all the time.'

I said that I was feeling okay. 'I should go. Bye, Sylvia.'

'I'll see you soon,' she said gently, confidently.

I put the snacks within easy reach of the table and refilled Frida's glass of water.

'The physio will come tomorrow,' she said. 'Then a few more weeks of exercises at home.'

'And then the pool,' I said.

Frida smiled. 'You must keep swimming. I'm going to swim all next winter. I want to push myself. I will be cold and my body will learn to be cold.'

'As long as you're feeling good. You need time to get better.'

She yawned and closed her eyes. In a quiet voice she said, 'Don't doubt me.'

I stayed late that evening.

'My sick leg is so ugly,' Frida kept repeating.

I tried to reassure her.

'My sick leg is so ugly.' She said it again and again. 'I hate this,' she said.

The hospital started to wind down for the evening; the staff changed shifts after dinner, the lights were lowered.

Frida moved her arms and her upper torso lifted slightly, as if she were a restless baby. She moaned, 'My leg. It needs to move, help me move it.'

I asked the night nurse for some cold cream and I pulled off the white sheet covering her body. Lifting the gown to her hip, careful of the wound, I massaged the thick cream over her leg, from the thigh down to the knee. She sighed, relieved, and was soon asleep.

I returned after work the following day. I helped her walk to the bathroom. She was in there a long time. When she finally emerged she had a strained, teary look on her face. She said, 'I'm scared of knocking the scar with my hand or my clothes and tearing off the stitches, opening the wound.'

I helped her back to bed.

She was angry at me when I held out a muesli bar. 'I can feed myself. I'm not so feeble, am I?'

I helped Frida home in a taxi. She was walking well, just one crutch to support her, *so I don't freak out*, she said, and she assured me she would be fine on her own for a few days.

'You look like you need some rest,' she said to me for the first time.

I went straight from her house to work. I realised how exhausted I felt.

And it's true that in the weeks after Frida's operation, I felt increasingly unwell again. This is repetitive, good and bad and well and sick and again, but I must speak truthfully. I spent another week of nights awake, the days were all rib and neck, bones composed the hours, muscle became mood. I wanted to say to Tomasz, *I can't turn to look at you.* Conversations reached me as if through water.

Through the nights, immunity flooded my thoughts. I thought of Frida, those nights in her hospital bed. Those pain hours were full of questions. Immunity, autoimmunity, self-immune. Inflammation, burning self. And where does all this heat come from? A disgusting hot factory burning up my insides. When I had thoughts like this, Tomasz was far from me; his sleeping left me alone on an island.

Such diseases are the body upon the body. Sharpening by breathing a blade that both makes and saves a victim. A body. This was not what we were supposed to do. Hour after hour. Only my eyelids and the city cats screeching their way to safety. I was a sheet laid over coals; I found sleep in mean corners.

Frida and Sylvia, Sylvia and Frida. I did not seek the doppelgänger. I have said this. The only conclusion I can offer is that doubling, tripling, insofar as my own narrative was concerned, might be a vehicle for rational examination of the self.

A few weeks after her surgery, the doctor told Frida she could return to the pool.

'There are many thresholds, I'm learning, with a body that is bad and then good and then bad again,' she said. 'I was ready for things and then I had to wait for things. I was ready for surgery. I was ready to return home. Now I'm ready for the pool again.'

She went back to the hydrotherapy pool in Fitzroy. I waited for her at the entrance to the hospital building around the corner, near the kiosk where nurses ate their lunch from plastic containers. It felt like a long time since I had been there; I almost felt nostalgic for that time meant for healing.

'Are you in a hurry?' I asked her.

We went for coffee at the cafe inside the hospital.

'Here we are all over again,' said Frida. 'All over again in this body.'

We met at the Sea Baths in what would be our last visit there together. St Kilda was crowded; some festival or event along the Esplanade, near the foreshore and the Palais Theatre. After some time in the hydrotherapy spa and then a few laps of the pool, we opened the door onto the sand. Beneath a slate-grey sky we paddled and floated in the salty shallows.

We showed each other our scars, both on the upper leg, alongside the pubic line. The ghosts of wounds now healed or healing. Frida's was a vivid red-brown line, a young scar, mine an old, milky vein. I told her how, after the surgery, because the doctor had needed to cut the nerve on my leg to reach the joint beneath, I couldn't feel the skin on my upper thigh. But I could feel it with my hand. It was a strange, half-sided version of myself. 'I feel the same thing,' she said, 'or I feel the same absence.' She smiled, and her delight at the truth of this phrasing made her seem for a moment so very like Sylvia.

'I don't like this version of me,' Frida said. 'Often these days I don't feel like swimming.' Frida looked at me, her wet hair plastered over her scalp. 'I think I miss the hospital.'

Her voice was hushed, as though she were ashamed. 'What does that even mean? What is wrong with me?'

'It's the safety of it,' I said. 'Convalescence. You're healing, cared for, do not need to go outside. For once, to rest is normal.'

'I guess you're right,' she said, leaning back into the salt water, letting it hold her up. 'The hospital and its routine, the safety of its control. It surprises me, still, how much it comforted me.'

'And there is no shame in this,' I said. 'We turn inwards. We don't need to go anywhere, we are advised not to go outside.' My voice, I realised, spoke of this with reverence.

We went inside to sit in the steam room, our bodies parallel.

She said, 'Look at us, how we sweat, how we shine.'

Back at her apartment, Frida was restless. I could not tell if she was sick of me or scared that I would leave. I convinced her to take painkillers. She gave in, took two white tablets of paracetamol. I wanted her to rest. Perhaps she didn't know how to be still; it was not in her self-told story of recovery.

'I'm awful,' she said. 'I just want to lie down and stare at the wall, stare at the ceiling, lie here with my hands turned up and feel light. A weightless statue. I sound ridiculous.'

'Let your body relax,' I said. 'You're so high-strung with all the pain. Let your brain rest a little.'

'I don't want to rely on them. The pills. I'm worried I will.'

'You need to rest.'

'You're obsessed,' she said. 'You're so devout about rest.'

'Try not to distrust it. I have tried. I am trying. It's not so bad; it doesn't make you bad.'

She looked at me, an uncertain smile forming. She asked, 'What is the cost of control, and what are its rewards?' She paused and then continued in a conspiratorial, smiling way. 'Control is beautiful to me. It is admirable, desirable, a remarkable structure, a safety, an edifice on a peak. Languishing, lack of control, laziness—I hate them, I can't distinguish between them. Exercise and balance, more and more of it. For every problem, a cure is in control.' Her chest rose and fell a little too fast.

'There isn't a cure, Frida.'

'I know,' she said. Her breathing slowed. 'I know. You know I love you?'

I told Frida I loved her too.

I made us tea and she lay on the couch. I put a blanket over her. The sea air floated in through the open window. The dusky sun brightened the balcony briefly. I walked over the patterned floorboards, their repetition, tidal, walking into or out of the ocean. Frida closed her eyes.

From the window, looking at my reflection I said, 'Maybe one day you can meet my friend Sylvia.'

Frida was quiet, her face as impassive as a statue. She seemed, finally, to be sleeping.

At our house in Parkville I had coffee on the balcony and then walked the circle of native grasses in Royal Park. The city ahead of me: as though resurrected from beneath the sea, the buildings covered in fish scales, windows shining and reflective. Rose-gold new day.

There she was, just a little way along the path adjacent to mine, leading to the circle of grasses. Sylvia. I didn't know if I wanted to see her. But of course she was there, walking slowly.

'I feel sick today,' I told her.

'You are, and so am I. We are.'

'What's happening to your fingers?'

Sylvia pulled up the thick woollen sleeves that she always held so tightly, and took off her gloves.

'I cannot fix these bones,' she said. Her knuckles and wrists were swollen red bulbs. She took my fingers in hers and said, 'I cannot fix these bones.'

I touched her knuckles and said, 'I cannot fix these bones.'

When she asked me, 'Do you like being my mirror, and me being your mirror?' I told her the truth: I'd wanted to be Frida and Frida only.

'Sometimes I've wanted to forget you,' I said. But I stayed truthful to Sylvia, said I knew that I was her and she was my looking glass and I couldn't very well extract her from my life, as though she was just a character in a book I was writing, who would exit the room forever. I asked her, asked Sylvia, if she would come to the pool with me. She smiled, almost mischievous, and touched my shoulder.

I went to the outdoor pool at the Carlton Baths. It was late spring and the days were sunny, the mornings cold. I liked it because there were no great distances to walk, objectively speaking, from the changing rooms to the pool, or from the pool to the seat where I put my towel and flip-flops. And I liked the grounds bordered by an attractive red-brick wall, the streets beyond lined with London plane trees.

I was the first one in the pool. It was a crisp, sunny morning. The synthesis of the early cold air and the heat of the solar-warmed pool formed a layer of steam just above the surface of the water. I shuddered a moment at the cold and then stepped into the warmth. The weightless return again and again.

Soon a man and then a woman entered the pool, each taking a lane. Their limbs rose through the steaming white surface of the water as though emerging from a primordial substance, a birth of adulthood into a new way of being, as if we were all engaged in some secular baptismal ritual on this leafy suburban morning. Emergence, emergence. To me it was beautiful.

I rested at the end of the lane, following the flight of a bird overhead. Some days I hurt and others I felt better and then I would hurt again.

I looked over as another woman walked towards the pool. The white glare off the water nearly obliterated her from view. She had long blonde-auburn hair that she was just then tying up as she stood at the top step. She tucked her hair up into a dark red swimming cap. Unsteady, she held the handrail and moved slowly down the steps until the water covered her legs, her waist. She brought her arms out to her sides, a winged movement, testing the surface, then started to walk towards my lane. She ducked under the rope and emerged, dripping in the morning steam. The momentum of the water nudging my breasts and arms and shoulders in miniscule waves, from the movement of her own body, shook me unaccountably.

'Sylvia.'

We moved, Tomasz and I, the following winter. A house of our own, a single storey. The house does not have a balcony. Now that we've left the old terrace share house, I miss the height. I miss the view from the balcony. I would have thought that being so close to the ground is good for humans, but I long for the height and distance.

I have not seen Frida and Sylvia. Since we moved, I have not seen them once. But of course, now I go to different pools to swim: the outdoor pool in North Melbourne that is flecked in autumn with yellow leaves like sleeping fish, and then, in winter, the pool past the racecourse and the showgrounds. It is nothing like the salt of the Sea Baths. They are quite far from me now. And now I walk in different places, along the old cattle stock route down to the river, always involving a busy road or two, gaping intersections that bring out all kinds of terror and confidence in me, from one day to the next.

I never asked for their phone numbers. They never had mine. They do not exist online in any profile or identity. I know that I could go to Royal Park, I could go to the Sea Baths. Of course I could. I have found things to love about this new place. I fear that I am less devout about some things now, and therefore the scraps of self-knowledge I gathered as I recovered in those months after the hospital have lost importance or relevance to me. It is perhaps as simple as saying: the person I was in front of each of them, I am not anymore. The pendulum I felt ticking back and forth between them no longer exists. No longer am I Frida. No longer am I Sylvia. I am simply no longer them.

WORKS QUOTED

The passage discussing J.M. Coetzee on Dostoyevsky is from Eleanor Wachtel's interview with Coetzee, published in *Brick Literary Journal*, Issue 67, Spring 2001, p. 45.

The quote by Susan Sontag 'My point is that illness is *not* a metaphor', is from her book *Illness as Metaphor*, Farrar, Straus and Giroux, New York, 1978, p. 3.

The section on Francesca Woodman refers to Arthur C. Danto's article 'Darkness Visible', which appeared in *The Nation*, 28 October, 2004, and quotes from Marco Pierini's essay 'Dialogue of One', translated from Italian by Piccia Neri, which appears in *Francesca Woodman*, edited by Marco Pierini, Silvana Editoriale, Milan, 2010, p. 41.

The lines 'I shall never get out of this!' and 'She was shaped just the way I was' are taken from Sylvia Plath's poem 'In Plaster', from her *Collected Poems*. I wish to thank Faber and Faber Ltd for permission to use these lines.

ACKNOWLEDGEMENTS

I live and work in Naarm/Melbourne, on unceded lands belonging to the Wurundjeri and Boonwurrung Peoples of the Eastern Kulin Nation, and I would like to pay my respects to their Elders past and present. I acknowledge First Nations cultures across Australia, their ongoing connection to Country and thriving storytelling traditions.

My thanks to the wonderful Robert Watkins for your support and enthusiasm for this book. Thanks to Ali Lavau—how lucky I am to work on three books with you, and to James Kellow, Alisa Ahmed, Bec Hamilton and the Ultimo Press team. Thanks to Clare Forster, Allison Colpoys for the beautiful cover, Anna MacDonald, and to Varuna Writers' House for supporting me to work on this book with the Eleanor Dark Fellowship. Thank you to Angela, Isabel, Katie and Rheny. And to Miles Allinson, Claire Thomas, Laura McPhee-Browne and Oliver Mol—thank you all for your generous words.

My love and thanks to my family and to Marcin, for nurturing not only a book about chronic illness but being there for a life with it. Special gratitude to the Klaubers in New York and most of all to Maya—whose friendship has helped this book come to be.

Katherine Brabon is the author of the novels *The Memory Artist* and *The Shut Ins*. Her work has been awarded *The Australian*/Vogel's Literary Award and the David Harold Tribe Fiction Award, and nominated for the Christina Stead Prize, the Voss Literary Prize and the ALS Gold Medal. She lives in Naarm/Melbourne.